The Solitary Rose

by

Anne Rollins

The Solitary Rose

Cover Art by *Debbie Taylor*

The Wild Rose Press, Inc.
PO Box 708
Adams Basin, NY 14410-0708
Visit us at www.thewildrosepress.com

Publishing History
First Edition, 2023
Trade Paperback ISBN 978-1-5092-5053-0
Digital ISBN 978-1-5092-5054-7

Published in the United States of America

This argument maddened him. He wanted to bury his head under a pillow and forget it had ever happened. "I am not engaged to you, I am not married to you, and I will not sell my virtue. You will have to find someone else to experiment on. The only woman I am planning on bedding is my wife. You don't want to marry me, do you? Then this conversation is over."

Miss Ainsworth narrowed her eyes. She lifted one arm so she could rest her chin on her hand as she looked at Henry. Henry grew nervous. He could not imagine what she was going to try next, but from the look on her face, she was not ready to throw down her arms. He felt even more certain of that when a slow smile crossed her bewitching lips. Something about that smile made the hairs on his arms stand up straight.

"Very well, Mr. Dawson," she said. "You win."

Henry blinked. If he had won, why was she smiling like the proverbial cat who had stolen the cream? "What have I won?" he asked cautiously.

"My hand in marriage, of course," she replied. "I accept your proposal. We are betrothed now."

Dedication

This one is dedicated to John.
Thank you for supporting my writing!

Chapter One

England, May 1814

Henry Dawson squinted at the name on the placard outside the stately-looking three-story stone building. It read "Smith and Marston, Solicitors." He dropped his gaze back to the letter in his hand to confirm the address. He had been afraid the whole thing was some sort of swindle or trick, but the respectability of the address had convinced him to at least walk by. Now that he was here, looking up at the office building, he had a hard time believing he was being swindled. He had asked a few people, and no one had ever heard anything the least bit disreputable about Smith or Marston. On the contrary, they were known to be very respectable solicitors, patronized by some of the best families in York.

"Excuse me." A young man with a pencil tucked behind his ear opened the door and poked his head out. "Are you Mr. Dawson?"

"Yes, I am he," Henry replied nervously. There seemed to be no point in denying it. The street was nearly empty of foot traffic at the moment. No one could overhear him.

"Mr. Marston is waiting for you, sir. Please come in."

Henry had not made up his mind about whether he should keep the appointment, but now there seemed to be no help for it. He followed the clerk into the building and into a snug office at the back of the ground floor. The sign on the door labeled this Mr. Marston's office, and the man behind the desk must be Marston himself.

Mr. Marston, who looked to be in his fifties, had a snub nose and ruddy cheeks. He looked Henry up and down, squinting at him a little, then nodded. "Please take a seat, Mr. Dawson. I'm sure you're wondering why I've called you here."

"Er, you said you know something that might be to my advantage?" Henry suggested, getting straight to the point.

He found those words highly suspicious. How many desperate men in the past had been lured into trouble with just such a phrase? But an apothecary's assistant with two younger siblings and a widowed mother to support could not afford to overlook anything that might be to his advantage. To be sure, his mother had her own fortune to rely on, but it did not provide enough for all her needs or wants.

"Indeed." Mr. Marston fixed him with a piercing look. "Mind you, if you have come here hoping to hear that a long-lost uncle left you a fortune, I am afraid you will be disappointed. It is nothing like that."

"Oh, I see." Henry hoped that his face did not reveal how crushed he felt. He *had* hoped that a legacy lay at the root of this unexpected invitation. He could have used even the smallest gift from a long-lost uncle. He had, in fact, wracked his brains trying to think of anyone who might conceivably have died and left him something.

"Still, if things work out as I hope, this may solve your financial difficulties."

"Er, my financial difficulties?" Henry tried to assume an expression of confusion, as if he had never in his sheltered life even heard of financial difficulties.

"You have a sister and a brother who attend boarding school, correct? And I believe your mother's income does not cover the costs of their education." Mr. Marston peered over his spectacles at Henry. "That is why you left Cambridge to work in an apothecary shop, is it not?"

"Well, yes." Henry's face burned with shame. "But I don't know how you know all this."

"I have been gathering information about you ever since you were recommended to us by a university friend of yours."

"Recommended for what, precisely?" Henry asked, again trying to get to the heart of the matter. He wanted to know what this was all about.

"For a very unusual position," Mr. Marston explained. "Nominally, you would be the librarian at Westwinds. It is a manor house in the North Riding, near Whitby. But your real task—well, I will leave that to Mr. Ainsworth to explain. My role here is just to verify some facts before we proceed. First, I am required to ask if you are a churchgoer?"

"Yes, I am." Henry blinked in confusion, not seeing the import of such a question. His mother was very devout, and she had instilled strong principles in all her children. But he had not expected that to matter to anyone.

"How often do you drink to excess?"

"What kind of question is that?" Henry asked, getting irritated.

Mr. Marston smiled tightly. "I have been given a list

of questions to ask you. Most of them are yes or no questions, so they ought to be simple enough for you to answer. How often do you drink to excess?"

"Never, since college. I do not like being drunk." Or, more accurately, he did not like the way he felt the morning after getting foxed. "I like a glass of wine with my dinner, just like anyone else, but I don't drink much." He had a taste for brandy, but could not afford to indulge it, good brandy being expensive and his salary being small.

Mr. Marston nodded and made a note about that. "Have you any serious health problems? Any impairments?"

Henry shrugged. "I am left-handed, does that count?"

"That does not count." The frown on Mr. Marston's face suggested that he was not amused. "Being left-handed is thought to be a sign of luck for magicians, is it not?"

"Yes, but I only have a little magic, you know," Henry said apologetically. "I can work small, simple sorceries. Nothing complicated or large."

Sorcery was a convenient gift, as it did not require ingredients to work magic, but Henry's abilities were quite limited. His magic did at least allow him to mix magical medicines in the apothecary shop, so he had come to appreciate it more over the last two years.

"And you can shield your mind from empaths and telepaths?" Mr. Marston's body tensed strangely at this question.

"Oh, yes, I do that very well." Henry had a friend at university—in his own college, in fact—who was an annoyingly powerful empath with poor ethics. Henry had developed his mental shields in order to keep Thompson out of his head. He had been the best in his college at it. "That is practically my only accomplishment," he admitted, smiling a little.

Mr. Marston's face did not relax a bit. Once again, he did not seem amused. "Let me tell you, young man, it is that accomplishment that makes you ideal for this position."

"It is?" Henry did not see how that could be relevant.

"Yes." The solicitor nodded solemnly. "If you accept this position, you will be working alongside a very powerful empath. But Mr. Ainsworth will explain more about that. I must continue with the interview. Please describe your relations with the fairer sex."

"Excuse me?" Once again, Henry's fair face burned with embarrassment. "What does that have to do with anything?"

"It is an extremely vital question!" Mr. Marston had been recording Henry's answers in a small notebook, but now he tapped his quill against the desk, as if growing irritated.

"I have no relations with the fairer sex!" Henry said indignantly.

"No fiancée? No sweetheart?"

"No, of course not." Henry sighed and looked down at the desk. There had been Mary Kingsley, once upon a time, but that was long since over.

To his horror, Mr. Marston next asked, "You were quite close to a Miss Mary Kingsley two years ago. Please describe your acquaintanceship with her."

"How do you know that?" Henry demanded. Was someone spying on him? Why? He could imagine nothing that anyone could gain by spying on him.

"I have done my research, like a good solicitor. Please answer the question, Mr. Dawson." Mr. Marston continued to tap his quill pen on his desk impatiently.

"I suppose Miss Kingsley and I were sweethearts once," Henry admitted. "That is, I courted her, and she seemed to prefer me. But then my father…that is to say, I became ineligible. I broke things off, and she married someone else. That is all there is to it. We were never formally betrothed." He had been heartbroken about it once, but Mary must not have been inconsolable, given that she married a wealthy landowner only three months after he bid her farewell.

"And how far did your relations with her progress while you were courting her?"

Henry's back straightened in shock. "I have no idea what you mean."

"Oh, I believe you do, Mr. Dawson. All our reports suggest that you are an intelligent man. How intimate were you with Miss Kingsley while you were courting with her?"

"If you mean to suggest that I committed any impropriety with her, that is a slander against an innocent lady," Henry snapped. "All I did was waltz with her a few times and kiss her under the mistletoe once." Now the redness of his face was due as much to anger as to embarrassment. "These questions are most improper!"

Mr. Marston sighed. He ran a hand over his balding head and looked down at the notes on his desk as if he, too, found the interview humiliating. "I believe you will better understand the motive behind them once your future employer discusses the true nature of your position. In any case, I must embarrass you further by asking whether you frequent brothels?"

"Of course not!" Henry snapped. "I couldn't afford to do that even if I wanted to!" He could not even afford to dine at a chop house this month, which would have been much more satisfying. (Probably.)

"Yes, quite." The corner of Mr. Marston's mouth twitched. "The question is, would you do it if you could afford it?"

Henry's jaw dropped open. There were things that one gentleman simply never asked another…and yet here sat Mr. Marston, calmly asking such forbidden questions. He swallowed nervously and admitted the truth.

"No, I wouldn't. My mother would kill me if I did something like that and she found out. She raised me to be a strict churchman, you know."

She had, in fact, wanted Henry to be a clergyman. He sometimes wished that he had pursued that career. Being a curate would not have paid more than being an assistant in an apothecary shop, but it would have given him a much more respectable social position. A clergyman was a gentleman.

Mr. Marston nodded and jotted something down in his notebook. "What are your views on parenthood, Mr. Dawson?"

"I don't have any views on parenthood," he retorted, still feeling disgruntled by the personal nature of these interrogations. "Not being married. And before you ask, I don't have any illegitimate children." He could be certain of that. One had to do more than kiss a girl to become a father.

"Young man, use your imagination a little. If you were a parent, how would you treat your children?" Mr. Marston's voice sounded cranky, as if he, too, were growing irritated by the interview.

Henry sighed. This was the most pointless question he had ever been asked. Most likely he would never be able to afford to marry. "If I had children, I would want to spend time reading to them, and, ah, playing with them." What did one do with children? He tried to remember his childhood, but it seemed a lifetime ago. So much about his life had changed in the last two years. "Playing ball and charades and whatnot. And of course, I would want them to be well-educated, and, er, religious and all that. And kind," he added as an afterthought. He hoped that none of his children would grow up to be bullies or be cruel to animals.

"What are your views on the education of females?" Mr. Marston asked him next. The question did not surprise him. Henry was just relieved it was nothing more personal.

"I don't have any views on the education of females."

"But you sent your sister to boarding school," Mr. Marston pointed out.

"My mother's health prevents her from teaching her herself." Henry's mother had never completely recovered from the shock of his father's death and the loss of their family estate, Switherton. "I want Eliza to have a good education, so she has options." Her background would qualify her to be a governess or schoolteacher someday, if she were properly educated. Given the family's financial losses, it was important for her to be independent.

"So, would it be fair to say that you believe girls deserve an education as much as boys?"

"I suppose so." He had never put it that way himself,

but he agreed that Eliza deserved a good education as much as Jasper did.

"Excellent. One last question, Mr. Dawson. What do you think about the use of physical discipline against wives or children?"

"Against *wives*?" Henry's jaw dropped. The very nature of the question shocked him. "What man uses physical discipline against his wife?"

"A great many men, unfortunately," Mr. Marston said sadly, "as the law allows it. I take it you do not approve?" He looked down at his desk, so that Henry could not read his expression.

"Of course not!" Henry said indignantly. "A gentleman should never hurt anyone, especially not a woman or a child."

At this, Mr. Marston looked up at Henry very keenly, his eyes narrowed. "You would not spank or switch your children, then?"

"No, that was not how I was raised." He had gotten a whipping or two at school, but that happened to all boys, and it was, so far as he knew, unavoidable. All schools he had heard of used corporal punishment. "Really, what is the purpose behind these questions?"

"I believe you are about to find out, Mr. Dawson, as you have answered them all in a satisfactory manner. But in the meantime, my clerk will show you to a waiting room where you can have some refreshments. You look, if you will pardon me, like you have not been eating well."

Henry had not thought that his face could turn any redder, but it did. He had *not* been eating well, because Jasper had had to have a tooth drawn by the dentist and the cost of sending him to London had been enormous.

Naturally, Mother had appealed to Henry for help. As a result, he was more than usually short on funds this month.

"Thank you, sir." He would have liked to indignantly turn down the offer of refreshments, but he could not, because all he had had for breakfast was a slice of toast.

His wait allowed him time to drink two cups of tea and eat most of a plate of biscuits and cheese. He wondered where the clerk had gotten the cheese from. Did the solicitor keep it in his office? If so, why? But he did not ask. He merely ate it and found it very good. If he had had a glass of hock to go with it, it would have been a perfect meal. But no one offered him any wine, and perhaps that was just as well.

He must have waited for nearly half an hour before the clerk returned and politely said, "If you will step this way, sir?"

Henry stepped that way, wondering what god-awful interrogation he would face next. The clerk led him back to Mr. Marston's private office, but Mr. Marston was gone. Instead, a tall, slender man with dark brown hair sat behind the desk.

"Mr. Ainsworth, may I introduce you to Mr. Dawson?" With no other word of explanation, the clerk left Henry alone with the stranger.

The gentleman stood and nodded his head cordially to Henry. Henry was used to being taller than most people he met, but this Mr. Ainsworth was perhaps only an inch shorter than he was.

"How do you do, Mr. Dawson? I am very pleased to meet you, after what Mr. Marston tells me of you."

Henry nodded politely, though this greeting puzzled

him. "How do you do?"

Mr. Ainsworth gestured to the seat in front of the desk and Henry sat down in it for the second time that day, wondering if Mr. Ainsworth also intended to ask him a series of impertinent personal questions.

But Mr. Ainsworth took his own seat and smiled reassuringly. "I am sure you are very confused about the nature of this interview. But I can explain everything."

"Please do," Henry said. "For I must say that I have never been so embarrassed in a job interview in all my life."

Mr. Ainsworth chuckled. "No, I suppose not. But then, this isn't really a job interview."

"It isn't? I thought there was a position..." Confused, Henry did not continue. Wasn't that what this was about? "Didn't Mr. Marston say something about a library?"

"Oh, yes. That's the excuse we're using to send you to Westwinds. Nominally, you will be in charge of cataloguing my late father's library on magic. It is certainly in need of being sorted, and my niece cannot do it because the dust gives her a catarrh. We are prepared to pay you triple your current quarterly salary to do this work."

Henry sat up straighter at that part. Mr. Ainsworth nodded and smiled before he continued. "If all you accomplish during your stay this summer is sorting the library, I will be most grateful. But I hope you will do something of much more importance." He steepled his fingers together and leaned forward slightly, studying Henry intently.

"Yes?" Henry prompted. A faint uneasiness stirred in his gut, and he clasped his hands together nervously.

This must be the catch. "What is the other task?" It must be something difficult or unpleasant, he guessed, from the solemn look on Mr. Ainsworth's face.

But Mr. Ainsworth unexpectedly smiled. "It is a matter of great personal importance to me. You see, Mr. Dawson, I hope that you will woo and marry my niece."

Chapter Two

Emma Ainsworth lay in the hayloft of the old stone barn, listening to the shuffle and stamp of the milk cows below. Late afternoon sun slanted through the open window at the end of the loft. The milkmaid was already at work, singing to herself as she moved from cow to cow. The milkmaid had a pleasant voice, and her mind was full of pleasant thoughts, so even though she had poor mental shields, Emma did not mind her company. In fact, it made a soothing backdrop to her own rather boring task.

There! Something stirred! She held her breath, afraid to ruin the moment. Sure enough, a tiny shape toddled out from between two bales of hay. She sighed in relief. The kittens were older than she had thought, walking and exploring already. They were likely old enough to be reared on bowls of milk, until they were ready for fish. Perhaps they were already old enough for solids.

Emma got to her feet. The kitten startled and ran, which was convenient, as it ran back to its nest. She had to move a bale of hay aside, and there they were, five kittens, a mixture of orange, calico, and black. They wobbled about and mewed. Emma could not resist scooping one of them up and snuggling it. It wriggled in her grasp before it began to purr. At this age, domesticating the kittens should be easy.

"Miss Ainsworth?" Emma recognized the voice of Hattie, the upstairs maid. "Your uncle is here and wishes to see you."

"Uncle Elwood?" Emma said, surprised. He had sent no warning of his visit. "Hattie, can you let Purdy know that I found the orphaned kittens?" Their mother, an excellent mouser, had been killed yesterday, kicked in the head by a cranky milk cow. Emma had feared the kittens would starve. "They are old enough to feed, if one of his daughters wants to look after them. And if not, I can."

She guessed that one of Purdy's daughters would want to do it, though. He had three daughters, and all of them loved baby animals. They made a nuisance of themselves at calving time, wanting to cosset the new calves and weeping over the fate of the veal calves. They would love having a nest of kittens to raise.

And Emma would be on hand to help them in the unlikely event they needed help with the kittens. Children's minds were sometimes louder than those of adults, but children did not display as much hypocrisy and double-mindedness as adults did, so Emma did not mind their company. Their thoughts might be angry or rebellious, but their words generally matched their thoughts…until they grew old enough to be polite.

Emma scrambled down the ladder to where Hattie waited. "You might want to brush your dress off a bit, miss." Hattie giggled, but the smile on her face looked friendly rather than mocking. Nor did Emma pick up any mockery with her empathy.

Emma looked down. "Oh, yes." She absently swept the straw off her dress.

"Your uncle has a guest with him."

"He has a *what*?" Emma stopped in her tracks, horrified by this revelation. She knew of no guest who ought to have accompanied her uncle.

"A young gentleman. Ever so handsome!" Hattie beamed as if this were not terrible news.

To Hattie, the arrival of a handsome gentleman provided unexpected entertainment. It would give her something to talk about with the other servants in the house. But to Emma, it spelled disaster. Emma looked down at her dress more carefully this time, and what she saw made her heart sink. The dress had been shabby before she went crawling about in the hayloft. Now?

"I can't meet a guest looking like this! Please tell my uncle that I am going to change."

"Yes, miss, and mind you get the straw out of your hair, too," Hattie advised.

Emma went up to the first floor by the servant's stair rather than using the main staircase. She did not want to run any risk of being seen by her visitor in this faded dress from two summers ago, with straw in her hair, and no hat. No veil, either.

If it had been only Uncle Elwood, she would not have minded in the least. He would not have been offended at her appearing before him in untidy clothing. But a guest! A young male guest, too. She could not imagine why her uncle had not warned her about this visit. He generally did warn her before asking her to meet new people.

It was almost dinnertime, so Emma put on one of her dinner dresses, a pretty thing of rose-pink silk. She fumbled with the laces on her muddy boots, hurrying to replace them with slippers. Then a lace cape, and a veil. No one wore veils indoors, but Emma did not care. She preferred not to let strangers see her face.

She found Uncle Elwood in the drawing room, chatting companionably with a young man so handsome she was tempted to turn around and run back to the barn before he saw her. But it was already too late. He looked up and met her gaze across the room. He smiled an uncertain, almost shy smile, and got to his feet.

So did Uncle Elwood, who immediately made the necessary introductions. "Ah, yes. Emma, may I present Mr. Henry Dawson to you? Mr. Dawson, this is my niece, Miss Ainsworth."

"How do you do?" Mr. Dawson bowed politely.

He had golden hair, like some kind of sun-god, and he stood well over six feet tall. His shoulders were broader than Uncle Elwood's, and overall, Emma's first impression was that Mr. Dawson ought to be clad in a scarlet coat. He would have made a magnificent army officer. Besides, if he were in the army, he would be serving abroad, rather than standing in her drawing room, taking up so much space. He was quite the largest dinner guest she could remember having.

"I am pleased to meet you." Emma shot an accusatory look at Uncle Elwood, then remembered that he would not be able to interpret it since she had her veil on. "I was not expecting guests," she added, hating how stiff her voice sounded.

Would Mrs. Seymour be able to serve two more people at dinner? Emma had the impression that all they were to be served was the leftover mutton from yesterday. That would not do for a guest.

Emma heard a flurry of flustered thoughts coming down the hallway. She moved out of the doorway to take a seat on a chair some distance from Uncle Elwood and his unwanted guest. She had hardly sat down when Aunt Mary rushed into the room.

"Mr. Ainsworth!" Aunt Mary's voice sounded calm, but Emma could sense distress radiating from her. "We were not expecting you. And you have brought someone with you, I see." Though Emma could not read thoughts the way she could emotions, she guessed Aunt Mary worried about the dinner problem, too. She had already changed into her own evening gown.

"I am sorry for showing up without notice. But I have my reasons." Uncle Elwood gave Aunt Mary a Significant Look, though Emma had no idea what it meant. Aunt Mary's eyes widened, and she turned her head to stare at the guest. "Miss Barker, may I present Mr. Henry Dawson? Mr. Dawson, Miss Barker is my late brother's sister-in-law. She lives here with my niece in the capacity of, er, chaperone."

Aunt Mary beamed at the guest. "I am so very pleased to meet you, Mr. Dawson."

Emma narrowed her eyes at her aunt, puzzled. Aunt Mary's whole tone of mind had changed after that look exchanged with Uncle Elwood. Did she know something about this guest that Emma did not?

The suspicion lurked at the back of Emma's mind as she monitored the tenor of Aunt Mary's mind throughout dinner. She could never get a good reading on Uncle Elwood, because he had very strong magical shields. It was one of the things that made him such a good companion. Even if he were hurt or frightened, he did not inflict his fear or pain on Emma the way other people did.

Mr. Dawson was equally impossible to read. This was both a blessing and an annoyance. A blessing because it meant there was no danger of Emma picking up feelings she had rather not know about. But an annoyance because she could get no sense from him of why he was here or what he thought about during the meal. Or what he thought about her.

The worst thing about dining with guests was that she had to remove her veil in order to eat. She made sure to do so while she was looking down at her soup, so that she would not see the expression on Mr. Dawson's face when he saw her face for the first time.

Sometimes people looked shocked when they saw her. Sometimes they looked pitying. Other times, they looked past her with indifference, as if her smallpox scars meant that she lacked value in a world that ranked women based on physical beauty. She did not want to see any of these expressions on Mr. Dawson's face. At least, the strength of his shields preserved her from feeling any shock or disgust when he looked at her.

Apart from that, dinner went well. Emma had been right about yesterday's mutton making an appearance, but the fish was fresh, and Mrs. Seymour had made both a roast chicken and a steak pie. Emma watched Mr. Dawson eat, her eyes wide with fascination. She knew staring was bad manners, but she had never seen a human being consume that much food at one meal. Well, except for her Uncle Max, and it had given him the gout. Mr. Dawson did not appear to have the gout …yet.

Uncle Elwood sat at the head of the table, as he always did when present. Westwinds had been his childhood home, though it had been left to Emma, and he managed it for her. It made sense for him to take the master's chair. And Aunt Mary sat at the foot of the table. Emma might be the lady of the house, but she was happy to let her aunt play hostess in her place. That meant Emma sat across from Mr. Dawson. If the family followed formal dining etiquette, he would be expected to talk to her aunt rather than to her. But they did not sit on formality when there were so few people at table, and the conversation remained general.

Mr. Dawson had never been to Whitby, and he had many questions about the town. Emma was more than happy to let Aunt Mary answer them. She kept her own responses short and to the point. Since she did not know why Mr. Dawson was here, she did not know how to treat him.

After dinner, Aunt Mary led the way to the drawing room. She settled on the sofa and picked up her sewing basket. "Emma, I would like to see you treat Mr. Dawson more cordially."

"I have been perfectly polite." Emma sat in her favorite chair and picked up a book. Then she leaned over to trim the lamp. The days were getting longer, but she wanted to make sure she had enough light for reading.

"Polite, yes," Aunt Mary agreed. "But you could be …well, warmer. Kinder. More welcoming."

"Why should I welcome him?" Emma raised her eyebrows and looked Aunt Mary steadily in the eye.

Aunt Mary looked away and fumbled with the sewing in her hand. Emma narrowed her eyes and frowned. Her aunt was hiding something, she could tell that much. Her empathy did not allow her to tell what Aunt Mary hid, but there were other ways of finding things out.

"Because he is your uncle's guest." Aunt Mary looked down at the sewing in her lap.

She was making baby clothes for the Ladies' Aid society. There had been a militia stationed nearby eight months ago—Emma had had to sit through a good many uncomfortable dinners with officers interested only in her dowry—and now there were a number of unwed mothers about to deliver babies. While the vicar preached a sermon about chastity that was too little, too late, Aunt Mary and her friends devoted themselves to making booties and blankets for all the new arrivals. Emma had been trying her best to help them. Her sewing was not as good as her aunt's, so she had stuck to hemming blankets rather than anything more complicated.

"He is more than just a usual guest, isn't he?" Emma said matter-of-factly. Aunt Mary jumped visibly, and a wave of panic rolled off her, sweeping through the whole room. Emma caught her breath at the feeling. For a moment, she wanted to bolt out of the room. "Shields, Aunt Mary, please," she begged.

"I am so sorry, my dear," Aunt Mary said. "I will try harder." They both knew she would have limited success. Aunt Mary did not have the magical abilities Uncle Elwood did, and she had only a limited capacity to shield her emotions from Emma.

Aunt Mary had not answered Emma's question, but she didn't have to. Her panicked reaction was answer enough to Emma. There was something strange about this Mr. Dawson. Or at least about his visit. He might be a perfectly ordinary gentleman, but something was up.

When the gentlemen came in, Mr. Dawson sat in the chair next to Emma's and proceeded to try his best to charm her. He smiled at everything she said, laughed at the slightest witticism she uttered, and agreed to all her opinions. When she mentioned how much she had enjoyed *Sense and Sensibility*, he agreed. When she complained about Byron's *Childe Harolde*, he agreed the poem was subversive. She felt certain that if she had claimed puppies were inferior to kittens, he would have agreed just as readily, despite having already told some anecdotes about his old shooting dog.

Emma felt so sick she could have vomited. She answered as curtly as she could and tried to put a halt to his smooth charm with sharp glances and even sharper answers. Eventually he took the hint and moved from her side to sit by Aunt Mary. He spent the rest of the night conversing with Aunt Mary about the women's sewing circle and their charitable work. Emma had to grudgingly admit the questions he asked her aunt were intelligent ones, but that was all she could see in his favor.

The moment Mr. Dawson left the room, Emma cornered Uncle Elwood and demanded the truth. "He's here to court me, isn't he? Uncle, where do you *find* these fortune hunters?"

In truth, it probably wasn't that difficult to find them. Many families had younger sons at loose ends, on the hunt for an heiress. Some of them would even be willing to marry a girl as imperfect as Emma.

"He's not a fortune hunter!" Her uncle sighed and tried to smooth down his hair, though it had not been disarranged. She found it telling that he looked at the wall rather than meeting her gaze. "He's a very respectable young man with a small gift for magic. He has a classical education and some university training, so I thought he would be ideal for the task of sorting the library."

Emma considered this. It sounded plausible. The last

time Uncle Elwood had visited, they had spent some time discussing the need to catalogue the library. Emma had bemoaned the fact that she was always seized by sneezing fits and a runny nose when she spent too long in the room.

"If Mr. Dawson is only here to catalogue the library, why did he try so hard to charm me tonight?"

"Perhaps he is a lady's man." Her uncle said this with a straight face, until the corner of his mouth twitched, as if something about that statement amused him. "A good-looking gentleman like him is probably used to flirting with all the young ladies. I am sure he means nothing by it."

Emma scowled at this unsatisfying answer. "Tell him to flirt with Aunt Mary, then. I am not interested in flirtations. You know that."

"I will speak to him. But Emma—" Her uncle hesitated for a moment, as if choosing his words carefully. "Do be kind to him. He has had rather a hard life, and he needs this job. I don't want you to scare him away."

"Scare him away?" Emma crossed her arms in front of her chest and stared at her uncle.

"You know perfectly well you scared away that curate who visited us two years ago," her uncle reminded her. "And there was the officer last summer—"

"Uncle, if you would stop trying to make matches for me with impecunious bachelors in search of an heiress, I would stop trying to scare them away! I do not want an arranged marriage!" To her dismay, her voice wobbled. "I want no one to buy me a husband." Her throat tightened with pain. Or was it anger?

"It's not an arranged marriage if you both like each

other!" He threw his hands in the air in despair. Or possibly frustration.

Emma caught herself in the act of putting her thumb in her mouth to gnaw the nail. She forced herself to take the hand away and relax.

"In any case, Mr. Dawson is just here to catalogue the books. All I ask is that you be polite to him. You can do that, can't you?"

"Yes. If you are telling the truth." Normally, she could tell when people lied to her. But she could not read Uncle Elwood's emotions, and he had too much command over his facial expressions to give much away through visual cues. She had to take his word for it.

"That's my girl." Her uncle rested his hand on her shoulder, allowing her to sense his affection and concern. "Chin up. He will only be here for a few months, and then he will go back to York and you can pretend you never met him."

Emma nodded. She could not say all her suspicions were allayed, but she resolved to give Mr. Dawson a chance.

In the morning, Mr. Dawson behaved quite differently at breakfast than he had in the drawing room. Perhaps Uncle Elwood had warned him not to flirt with her. Instead of smiling so much or laughing at everything she said, he generally ignored her in favor of talking to Aunt Mary and Uncle Elwood about the history of the house. Emma could not help feeling piqued, as she knew as much about Westwinds as anyone else. She jumped in with bits of history that her grandfather had told her, from the family ghost story to the mystery of Great-Uncle Roger's treasure.

"Treasure?" Mr. Dawson smiled at this. This boyish

grin was a very different smile from the flirtatious one he had showed last night. "What sort of treasure? Pieces of eight? Precious jewels? Fragrant spices?"

"One must hope not spices," Uncle Elwood pointed out, "as they would be nothing but dust by now."

"I always hoped for jewels," Emma admitted. When she had been a girl, she had hankered for jewelry. Unlike some wealthy families, the Ainsworths did not have a bank full of heirloom jewels. Emma had inherited nothing from her mother but a simple pearl set, and when she was younger, she had felt this to be a shame.

"I think gold doubloons more likely, myself," Uncle Elwood said.

"Perhaps books of magic," Mr. Dawson suggested cheerfully. "Ancient tomes passed down from father to son!"

"With the secret to the elixir of life in one of them," Emma agreed.

Mr. Dawson smiled at her very pleasantly, and she smiled back, until she remembered the suspicious circumstances that brought him here. Then her eyes shifted as she studied Uncle Elwood's face for any indication of his purpose in hiring Mr. Dawson.

If Mr. Dawson was not another one of her uncle's matchmaking attempts, why was he so ridiculously good-looking? Handsomeness was not a requirement for a librarian. But it would be very like Uncle Elwood to think her head might be turned by a pretty face, particularly one that displayed such an engaging smile. Emma, knowing character and temperament were more important than good looks, found Mr. Dawson's classical features annoying rather than attractive. Or so she told herself.

But Uncle Elwood merely spread jam on his crumpet and chatted with Aunt Mary about mutual acquaintances. When his eyes met Emma's, the corners of his mouth curled up. He did not look smug, guilty, or secretive. Perhaps she ought not be so suspicious. All the same, she avoided speaking directly to the new librarian for the rest of the meal.

After breakfast, Uncle Elwood asked her to show Mr. Dawson the library. She was pleased to see Mr. Dawson's jaw drop when they walked in. "This used to be the chapel, we think," she explained. It had been her favorite room at Westwinds until she realized that it made her sick.

"I should say so." He turned his head to study the room, taking in its high ceiling and tall windows.

"Iconoclasts knocked out the stained glass," she added, "and of course they stripped the altar." But they could not destroy the gorgeous arches of the windows, nor could they change the soaring ceiling. The angels at the corners of the ceiling had, miraculously, been left unmolested. She hesitated, then told him one of the family secrets. "There is a body underneath the chapel, you know."

"A saint?" His eyes dropped to the paved floor, as if he could see through the marble to what lay beneath.

She shook her head. "The altar relic is long gone, along with the altar. The body belongs to whoever owned the house before we did." She smiled apologetically. "Ainsworths have lived here for less than two hundred years. We are newcomers."

He nodded, showing that he understood. "My family only had Switherton for about a century before we had to sell it." He shrugged. "We made our fortune in trade and we lost it in speculation. Easy come, easy go, I suppose." He smiled grimly.

"I am sorry." Emma meant it. She tried to imagine what it might be like to lose Westwinds, but she could barely fathom it. Nowhere else on earth could possibly feel like home.

"Perhaps my younger brother will restore the family fortunes." He spoke cheerfully, but his face still looked grim. "He is more talented than I am. Quite a magical prodigy. I can only work simple spells, myself."

She could hear regret in his voice, but she did not entirely understand it. Most people could not work magic at all, so he had nothing to be ashamed of.

"Are all of these books of magic, then?" His eyes wandered about the tall bookcases now.

She shook her head. "The near wall is full of books of general information, and a few novels." Not nearly enough novels for her taste, unfortunately. "The other three walls are full of spellbooks and books of magical theory. My grandfather was a bit of a gentleman scholar." She could not help a note of apology creeping into her voice. Poor Mr. Dawson had been assigned a ridiculous task. It would take months or years of work to catalogue the library. "Unfortunately, he arranged his books according to an order that he never bothered to explain to anyone else. And he kept no catalogue."

"And that is why I am here." Mr. Dawson nodded again. "Well, I certainly have my work cut out for me." He looked down at Emma and smiled ruefully. "Your uncle says you started doing some of the cataloguing?"

"Yes." Emma glanced away, pretending she was looking for something. Mr. Dawson was really much too handsome to make a comfortable houseguest. She did not even like to meet his eyes. They were a deep, dark blue that looked very well with the blue morning coat he wore.

She wondered if he had dressed on purpose to accentuate his eyes. Maybe he had not given up trying to flirt with her. Maybe he had just changed tactics. She had no beauty with which to entice an attractive man, but he might well be eager to repair his family's lost fortune by marrying her.

Still, he was ostensibly here to catalogue the library, so she might as well put him to work. She led him across the marble floor to the large table that occupied the middle of the room. Stacks of small leatherbound notebooks covered the surface.

"These are for recording the books, by author's last name. One entry per page."

"Really?" He picked up one of the catalogues and flipped through the pages. "Don't libraries usually cram as many entries as they can on a single page?"

"Yes, but this way there's room for additions. And you can read the writing more clearly." She flipped through the notebook until she found a perfect entry, one that contained the date of original publication as well as the edition number. "When possible, we like to note which edition we have, but that is not always possible."

"What does "M" mean?" he asked, pointing to another entry.

"Manuscript," she explained. "For a hand-lettered text. P is for printed. Most of the books date from after the invention of the printing press, but there are a few that are older."

"And where do I put the books after I record them?" he asked, looking around. She turned and pointed to the far wall, where some shelves had been cleared.

"These shelves all have numbers now." She led him to the nearest shelf so that he could see. "We're putting them in roughly alphabetical order, and you have to record the shelf number on the card."

"Oh." He looked around and rubbed his chin thoughtfully. "Where did you learn this system? I haven't seen anything quite like it. Not that I am much of a researcher."

"My uncle and I developed it." She had no experience with research libraries at all, never having been to school, but Uncle Elwood was very familiar them, and he had helped her develop a system that would make it easier to locate a book if anyone needed it.

Grandfather Ainsworth had been dead for five years, but magical researchers still wrote to Westwinds asking if he had X, Y, or Z manuscript that they could borrow. Emma found it difficult to answer these questions when she herself did not know the whole collection. Grandfather had, apparently, had the whole collection more or less memorized, though no one knew how that was possible.

"I suppose I had better get to work?" Mr. Dawson sounded doubtful. Or perhaps "overwhelmed" was the right word. He seemed to shrink a little in the face of the task before him.

"Yes," Emma said brightly, "you will be very busy this summer! I'm afraid I won't see much of you, since the books affect my breathing." Already, she could feel herself getting congested, just from standing in the room for so long. "Feel free to ask the cook for a snack if you get hungry. I will see you at dinner."

She fairly skipped out the door. If Uncle Elwood

was indeed trying to make a match for her, he had not thought the matter through. Mr. Dawson would spend all day in the library, where she could not go because the dust and mold made her ill. She would see him only at dinner and at breakfast. And after dinner… She frowned as she thought about that. Yes, the evening hours would be the challenge. She would just have to find tasks that took her out of the house in the evenings. Or that kept her too busy to talk. It should not be hard to do.

Yes, the summer would fly by, and soon enough Mr. Dawson would leave. Then she would have her house to herself. Emma hummed as she skipped on her way to the barnyard. Time to visit the Purdy children and see how that litter of kittens was doing.

Chapter Three

Henry, for his part, felt that Mr. Ainsworth had failed to properly prepare him for the task ahead. It was not that Mr. Ainsworth had said little about Emma's character. On the contrary, Mr. Ainsworth had said a great deal. He had talked at length about her powerful empathic abilities, and how they often led to her being overwhelmed in public situations, when the emotions of large groups of people oppressed her. He counseled Henry on the importance of keeping his mental shields up at all times, both for Emma's comfort and for Henry's privacy.

And he had talked very frankly about the scars Emma bore as a remnant of the smallpox epidemic that killed her parents when she was nine. He warned Henry not to stare or comment on Emma's face, advising him to simply look her in the eye and act as if there were nothing different about her.

From the things that Mr. Ainsworth had said, Henry had developed a picture of the Miss Ainsworth he thought he was to court. He imagined her as a shy, unobtrusive girl, a shrinking violet, in fact, whose empathic powers forced her to hide from the world. He hoped that, armed with his shielding ability, he might be able to get her to open up when other suitors had failed. Mr. Ainsworth had been open about the fact that Emma had rejected previous matches he had tried to make for her. Henry had assumed this was due to Emma's shyness.

He had been completely and utterly wrong. Wrong about everything from Emma's appearance to her personality. She did have scars from smallpox, true, a smattering of pockmarks deeper than acne scars on her cheeks and forehead. Still, those light marks of her illness seemed like minor blemishes in Henry's eyes. They did not change the charm of her heart-shaped face or her kissable-looking mouth. She had dark, lovely eyes and hair of a deep brunette. As for the rest of her—well, Henry had to look when he first saw her wearing a rather daringly cut dark-red evening dress at dinner the second night.

More importantly, Emma was no shrinking violet. She resembled nothing more than a feral barn cat, all claws and hissing. The first night, she made it very clear she did not like Henry and would not encourage his suit. Henry thought it best for him to go back to York and see if he could get his old job back before Mr. MacGregor replaced him. It had been hard to find decently paying work for which he was qualified. He did not want to have to start over.

After dinner on the second day of the visit, when he and Mr. Ainsworth were alone, he explained this plan to Mr. Ainsworth while they sipped claret in the dining room. Emma and her aunt had gone off to the drawing room to do whatever it was that ladies did on their own. Henry suspected they made fun of the gentlemen, but no one ever admitted this.

"Nonsense," Mr. Ainsworth said, when Henry proposed to go back to York. "You haven't even tried yet. Don't you have any rumgumption?"

"Is that a real word?" Henry had never heard it before.

"It certainly is, and I wish you would acquire some of it," Mr. Ainsworth grumbled. "You can't quit after only one day."

"She hates me. Are you sure she even wants to be married?" Henry narrowed his eyes and glared at Mr. Ainsworth. He was being rude, no doubt, but he felt that he and Mr. Ainsworth had gotten past the point of adhering to etiquette. When a man tries to bribe you to marry his niece, the normal rules of social conduct do not apply.

Mr. Ainsworth frowned and shook his head. "She doesn't hate you. She doesn't even know you. She is angry at me for trying to arrange a marriage for her."

"Then why are you doing it? What's in it for you?"

Henry expected to hear about some secret clause in the will that gave Emma's uncle more money if Emma married by a certain age. Mr. Ainsworth had been trying to make a match for his niece ever since she turned eighteen, and she was now twenty. No one persisted at a thankless task unless some reward was involved.

"I am trying to do it because for all she snarls at her suitors, she does want a family," Mr. Ainsworth explained. "If you could see her around children, you would understand. The steward who manages the home farm has three children, and she dotes on them."

"So?" Henry said ruthlessly. "What does that have to do with me?"

"If she wants children of her own," Mr. Ainsworth said, using the voice that adults use when talking to children or idiots, "she needs a husband. That is why I keep trying to arrange a marriage for her."

"Maybe she likes children, but not men," Henry suggested. There were women who preferred the company of other women, as he knew very well. One of his aunts had lived with her companion for decades, refusing all suitors. The two women kept pug dogs and seemed blissfully happy together. Perhaps that was what Emma needed. "Maybe you should find her a female companion instead of a husband."

Mr. Ainsworth groaned. "Did you or did you not see the way her eyes widened when she looked at you? I am very sure she likes handsome men as much as any girl."

"Please don't try to flatter me," Henry growled. "I saw the way she looked at me, all right. And let me tell you, if her mind magic could manipulate physical objects, her look would have shoved me out the door and halfway to York."

She had been more polite later, it was true. She had voluntarily spoken with him at breakfast today. But he felt certain that the glare with which she greeted him before dinner the first day reflected her true feelings.

"She isn't mad at you," Mr. Ainsworth repeated. "She is mad at me."

Henry was not sure that distinction was helpful, given the way Emma seemed to direct her animosity toward him. "Why don't you let her pick her own husband? She obviously does not want you to do it."

Mr. Ainsworth threw his hands up in despair, then rumpled his hair. "How could she ever meet a man? She never leaves the house! She doesn't even go to church. Believe me, I've tried ways of getting her to meet a suitor naturally. It doesn't work. And…you know, because of the smallpox, the only suitors who seem interested are fortune hunters." He sighed.

"Am I not a fortune hunter?"

It was, after all, the lure of money that had brought Henry all the way to Westwinds. He had given up a paying job for the mere chance of marrying an heiress. He was pretty sure that made him a scoundrel. If he'd had only himself to think about, he would not have done it. He had no desire to sell himself as a matrimonial partner. But for his brother and sister? He was willing to be ruthless for them.

"I have it on good authority that you are a decent, hardworking young man." Mr. Ainsworth glared back at Henry. His hair stood up on his head from being rumpled, his cravat had become creased, and he altogether presented a rather alarming appearance. "The very fact that you question your integrity is one of the signs that you *have* integrity."

"Wait, what?" Henry protested. "That makes no sense." He shook his head. He was not even going to bother trying to sort that out. Instead, he returned to the real issue. "Have you tried advertising?"

"Advertising?" Mr. Ainsworth stared at him in disbelief. He poured himself a second glass of wine and took a gulp while Henry explained.

"I knew a boy in school whose father met his mother through an advertisement in *The Times*. Why don't you let Miss Ainsworth advertise for a husband herself? That way she can stipulate what kind of man she wants. *If* she wants one at all." Henry poured himself a second glass of wine, too. He was drinking more than he usually did, but he felt that the occasion called for it.

"You know," Mr. Ainsworth said, "that might not be a bad idea."

Henry sat up straighter and put down his glass of

wine. Perhaps he didn't need to get foxed tonight after all. Perhaps Mr. Ainsworth would listen to reason. He watched while Mr. Ainsworth tapped his steepled fingers together, lost in thought.

"I believe I will try that next," Mr. Ainsworth concluded. "Thank you for the idea. But in the meantime, as you are already here, I really think you had better give it a real shot instead of running away."

Henry groaned. "I don't think of it as 'running away.' I think of it as a strategic retreat." He took a sip of his claret after all, wishing that it were port instead. He didn't even *like* claret.

"Stop trying to be clever," Mr. Ainsworth grumbled. "Next time, I'm picking a stupider suitor."

"Because an intellectual girl like your niece will naturally be attracted to such a man?" Henry rolled his eyes. "I wish you the best of luck in that venture, sir."

"I think," Mr. Ainsworth said, "you had better dispense with the formalities and call me Uncle Elwood, just as Emma does. And, Henry—*may* I call you Henry?"

"I think you are going to call me that whether I give you permission or not." Henry could not quite keep the irritation out of his voice.

"In any case, Henry, I'll make you a deal. If you can stick it out for a month—thirty days, starting today—I'll give you a hundred pounds in addition to the salary we already agreed on. Yours just for staying here for one month. Is that a deal?"

That was more than Henry's annual salary in the apothecary shop. "It's a deal," he said reluctantly. He could not afford to pass up that much money. "But, *Uncle Elwood,* I am merely going to do my job as a librarian. I make no promises about wooing your niece."

One might as well try to tame a wildcat.

"Understood." But Uncle Elwood already looked more cheerful. He even made an attempt to smooth his hair back down. "If nothing else, you will give the ladies some company for the summer. Speaking of which, we had better rejoin them in the drawing room."

Henry was not sure what he expected to find in the drawing room. Miss Ainsworth armed with knitting needles and prepared for battle? But, on the contrary, the women were laughing at something in a lady's journal when the gentlemen walked into the room. They put the magazine aside to chat for a few minutes.

Then Miss Ainsworth got up and played the pianoforte, at Uncle Elwood's request. After playing a few simple folk songs, she claimed she had letters to write, and begged to be excused. Henry watched as both her aunt and her uncle frowned over this, exchanging one of their frequent speaking looks, but they let her go.

Saturday and Sunday passed in much the same way. On Sunday, Henry dutifully accompanied Aunt Mary to church. He listened as a curate who looked younger than his own four-and-twenty years gave a terrible sermon, and he found himself wishing he could have stayed at Cambridge long enough to earn his degree and be ordained. He could have done much better than this Mr. Franklin!

After church, Aunt Mary introduced him to her friends, including most of the women over the age of forty in the parish. Some of the friends had daughters, though, and some of the daughters looked at Henry with far more interest than Miss Ainsworth had. Was it his imagination, or did those mothers seem awfully eager for Aunt Mary to introduce him to their daughters?

Henry smiled and bowed and prayed that he could avoid an entanglement. He could not afford a wife, which meant he could not afford a sweetheart, which meant that he would have to ignore the very pretty girl with black hair and coal-dark eyes who kept batting her eyelashes at him. Even if he had the income to marry, hadn't he practically promised himself to Miss Ainsworth? Or did that not count, since she clearly wanted no part of him?

In any case, he refused to commit to calling on any of the families who offered him invitations. Instead, he bashfully confessed that his work would probably keep him too busy to enjoy the very pleasant company of his neighbors. He hoped the reminder that he had to work for a living would make the mothers stop staring at him so speculatively.

"Are there no bachelors in this parish?" he whispered to Aunt Mary as they walked up the road that led back to Westwinds. The church lay only a mile from the manor house, so the family walked in good weather.

"Many of them went off to fight in the war." She gave Henry a thoughtful, measuring look, moving her gaze from his head to his feet. Nothing made Henry seem more overgrown than that sort of look, which always seemed to say that he was too tall, too broad, and altogether too much. "Have you ever considered being a soldier, young man? You would wear a scarlet coat very well."

Henry sighed. "My mother made me promise not to enlist." After his father's death, she had been terrified that something would happen to Henry, Jasper, or Eliza. When he had suggested the army as a possible career, she shot the idea down immediately.

Henry had no desire to be on the receiving end of a bullet, but he did wonder if the army might have suited him better than a job behind the counter. But he could not afford an officer's commission in a desirable regiment. He would have had to settle for one of the regiments that did not require a purchase. Probably if he had gone to fight, he would already be dead by now. On the whole, he preferred not being dead.

"Pity," Aunt Mary said, shaking her head. "I always did like a soldier." Henry's face began to burn and he guessed that he was turning scarlet. He had no idea how one should respond to that sort of comment. "When the militia was here last fall, I introduced Emma to all the officers, but she didn't take to any of them. And she refused to go when she was invited to a dance the officers hosted."

"That's a shame." Henry meant it sincerely. If Emma had fallen in love with a soldier, he would not be in this awkward situation. Everyone would be much happier. "Does Miss Ainsworth dance?" For some reason, he had trouble picturing this.

"She *can* dance," Aunt Mary said, "but she never does. Touching another person makes it easier to feel their emotions, you see. She prefers to avoid physical contact."

Henry blinked and shook his head in confusion. If that was the case, how was Miss Ainsworth supposed to marry anyone? Or rather, once married, how could she fulfill the duties of marriage? He opened his mouth to ask, then thought better of it. He didn't think he wanted to discuss that with someone else's maiden aunt. In fact, he wouldn't have wanted to discuss it with his own maiden aunt. It was none of his business, anyway. He only had to catalogue the books for a month and then collect his pay.

Miss Ainsworth might not go to church, but she spent her Sundays reading devotional literature, and the only songs she would play on the pianoforte that night were hymns. That must have been why one of the first questions in that bizarre interview had been about Henry's churchgoing habits. Evidently, Miss Ainsworth was very devout.

He learned from Aunt Mary that though Miss Ainsworth did not often leave the house, she sometimes joined the Ladies' Aid sewing circle when they worked on charitable projects. That was the only thing Henry discovered about her that day. He had little chance to learn more about Miss Ainsworth, because she seemed determined to ignore him as much as possible. After reflecting on it, he decided that she probably had the right idea. He spent most of Sunday evening talking to Aunt Mary, she spent most of the evening talking to Uncle Elwood, and neither of them talked to each other at all if they could help it.

This plan seemed to work well, until Uncle Elwood returned to York. He was a wizard of considerable skill whose warding and enchanting services were in high demand, so he could not spare the time for a long holiday at Westwinds. When Elwood left, the evenings after dinner became more fraught with tension. With only three people in the room, Henry and Miss Ainsworth could no longer avoid each other. They had to actually talk.

Chapter Four

It would have been easier to hate Mr. Dawson if he had not been both amiable and intelligent. These qualities, as Emma well knew, did not always coincide with each other. The officer her uncle had tried to set her up with last year had been attractive and kind but not at all bookish, seldom reading anything more intellectually stimulating than sporting periodicals. The curate the year before that, on the other hand, had been academically inclined but also hot-tempered, scolding the servants in a most un-Christian manner if they got something the least bit wrong. Mr. Dawson did not display any such flaws.

At first, she thought Mr. Dawson's cordial good manners were a careful act, intended to ensnare her. But as the days of his visit stretched into weeks, she had to reluctantly admit that he really was as kind and thoughtful as he seemed. He listened patiently when Aunt Mary told the same story over and over again, he treated all their few guests with politeness, and though the extremely busty downstairs maid kept casting eyes at him, he blithely ignored both her eyes and her bust. And, to his credit, he never again tried to flirt with Emma.

Uncle Elwood had chosen rather better this time than in the past—Emma had to give him that. But that did not change the reality of the situation. She had no idea what bargain Uncle Elwood had struck with Mr.

Dawson, but she felt certain there *was* a bargain. Mr. Dawson had not come to court her because he had fallen in love with her based on description alone, like in a fairy tale. He was here because she was an heiress and he needed money. And Emma would never marry a man who was interested only in her fortune.

In the meantime, though, here he was, a polite, intelligent young man who could shield his emotions from her detection and carry on a conversation with a roomful of elderly women from the Ladies' Aid so well that half of them wanted him to marry their daughters or granddaughters. Weathering the varied emotions projected by the members of the Society always exhausted Emma, but she found it particularly trying to hear their reactions as they pumped Aunt Mary for information about Mr. Dawson. Many of them were envious.

Emma had to admit that a person like Mr. Dawson did not often come into her orbit. Maybe she ought to make the best of it. So, a few weeks into his stay, she asked him if he liked to ride.

His eyes lit up. "Oh, yes! I used to have a smashing hunter. He was a bit barn shy, but once you got him out on the field, he was game to take any fence I pointed him at."

"What happened to him?" Aunt Mary asked.

Emma tried to give her aunt a warning look, fairly certain she knew the answer.

"We sold him when my father lost our fortune," Mr. Dawson said.

Emma liked that he made no attempt to hide the truth. Nor did he blush, stammer, or look away. He said it simply and matter-of-factly. His family had been rich once; now they were not.

"Oh, dear me. I forgot." Aunt Mary looked down at her knitting. "That must have been so very hard."

"It was not as hard as my father's death."

For the first time, Mr. Dawson let a hint of emotion escape his shields. Emma felt a brush of grief, anger, and shame welling up from him, just for a second. Then he sat up straighter and slammed his shields tightly shut again. She could no longer read anything at all from him.

But what she had caught from him had been powerful enough to make her feel sorry for him. Perhaps that was why she suggested, "We should go for a hack across country this Saturday. You can ride the horse Uncle Elwood usually uses."

"Really? I would like that. If the horse is up to my weight."

Emma looked him up and down, considering the matter. Yes, as heavy as he was, he must be hard to mount. But her uncle's gelding was both tall and heavy-boned. "I think Bastian will do well with you on the flat, but I wouldn't take him over fences."

"Splendid." He grinned at her. "I haven't ridden in a couple of years."

As she looked as his cheerful face, which had been brightened by something as simple as a horseback ride, something twisted in her heart for a moment. Pity, perhaps? Sympathy? It did not quite feel like that. In truth, Emma was often better at labeling other people's emotions than she was at identifying her own.

But on Saturday, a storm blew in. Emma stood with her guest in the barnyard, watching the clouds roil in the sky above.

"We shall have to cancel our ride," Mr. Dawson

said. He did not sound disappointed. Because of his shields, she could not sense disappointment radiating from him, either. But something about the set of his mouth suggested that it was a real blow. He took his working hours very seriously, so they would likely not get a chance to ride until next weekend.

"We could go for a short ride," she suggested. "Just across the north pasture and back, perhaps. We can always turn back if it starts to rain."

She was rewarded with another one of his boyish grins. "Yes, let's try that. I'm game. A little rain won't hurt, anyway."

Emma agreed. Neither they nor the horses would be the worse for a little water. But at the first rumble of thunder, an icy shard of panic wedged its way into Emma's heart.

"We need to go back," she called to Mr. Dawson. "Bastian sometimes shies at loud noises." She would never have suggested taking him out if she had thought there would be thunder.

"Very well," Mr. Dawson said.

They turned and made their way along the cowpath that led home. When they got within sight of the stables, the horses picked up their speed, happy to be returning to their stalls. Then a bolt of lightning cracked, seemingly right overhead, and Bastian shied and bolted. To her surprise, Mr. Dawson kept his seat. He had not exaggerated his riding ability.

Emma's heart began to pound, but she forced herself not to tense up too much. She did not want to frighten her mount, too. "Try turning him in circles," she called after Mr. Dawson. Probably he already knew what to do with a bolting horse. If he could keep his seat and keep hold of the reins—which he seemed to be doing—he might be in no danger.

Then Bastian tripped over something and went down. For once, Mr. Dawson dropped his shields entirely and she felt every bit of his fear and pain as he landed, striking his right leg at a horrible angle. Emma could not hear words from people's minds, but she guessed that he was cursing fluently.

She rode up to him and dismounted, though her mare, Minnie, danced around uneasily. Bastian's bolting had frightened her. Emma had to take a moment to soothe her before she could help Mr. Dawson up. She came up to him, intending to apologize, but he beat her to it.

"I am so very sorry," he said, "but I think I have lamed your uncle's horse. He is favoring his leg." His face was white with pain, and Emma thought he shook from pain and shock. He had stopped cursing, though.

"But you have hurt your leg, too." Emma looked down at his leg and nearly felt sick. Even with his high boots on, she could see that the leg was crooked.

"At least it is only my shin and not my femur," Mr. Dawson gasped.

But the waves of pain rolling off him were so powerful Emma had to back away so she could be sick in earnest. How was *he* not sick?

"Oh, dear God, I am so sorry. I forgot about my shields entirely."

And, to her amazement, he somehow snapped his mental shields back up. The pain that had been radiating from him ceased, and Emma was left with only her own shock to cope with.

"Do you think you could walk if I helped you?" she

suggested.

He gave her a dark look, beneath lowered brows. She sighed. She did not need her mind magic to interpret that look. He was in too much pain to hobble back to the house. And doing so would have damaged the broken leg further.

"I will ride for a surgeon." She glanced at Bastian and gulped. "And the farrier, I suppose." If Bastian had broken his leg, too, he might have to be put down.

Henry looked at Bastian, too, and his mouth twisted. "I am so sorry."

"It was not your fault," Emma said brusquely. "I was a fool to suggest a ride in stormy weather." At least, she was a fool to suggest taking Bastian, knowing that thunder spooked him. But none of the other saddle horses would have been up to Mr. Dawson's weight.

She met Purdy coming into the barnyard, and he proved to be more sensible than she was. "You'll need a wagon to get him home," he told her. "I'll hitch up the plow horses." Of course. Why had she not thought of that?

"Is it safe to move him with his leg broken?" she worried out loud.

"Better than leaving him outside in a rainstorm," Purdy opined. She had to agree.

She could have sent a messenger to fetch Mr. Higgins, but she felt that she had to do something to help, so she rode for him herself. She was lucky enough to catch him just as he returned to his surgery after a house call. His horse was still hitched to the gig, so he lost no time getting to Westwinds. She, on a fleet saddlehorse, still beat him there. By the time she got back, Mr. Dawson lay in his bed, cursing fluently. His leg must have been greatly pained during the process of moving him inside.

"I beg your pardon," he panted when he saw her in the doorway, still wearing her cherry-red riding habit. "I ought not use such language in front of a lady."

"I have heard curse words before." She waved away his apology. He had his shields clamped down tightly, so she could not feel his pain, but she could see it in the whiteness of his face and the sweat that dripped down his face.

And when Mr. Higgins and Purdy worked together to set the leg, poor Mr. Dawson dropped the shields entirely and she felt the pain of the bone being set back into place. She cowered in her own room, her hands clamped over her ears, though that could not shut out the pain. She found relief by leaving the house to check on Bastian, in the stable. The farrier had arrived and, most fortunately, thought Bastian's injury would heal entirely. He would not have to be put down after all.

By the time Emma returned to the house, Mr. Dawson had been sent to sleep with a dose of laudanum. Mr. Higgins was not optimistic about the broken leg.

"If you want my advice, ma'am," he said, "You should send for Dr. Thomas in Whitby. He is the nearest medical magician. It was a compound fracture, I'm afraid, and wounds like that often get infected. Dr. Thomas may be able to prevent infection, or burn it out if it sets in."

"Yes, of course, we will do that." Emma would have sent all the way to York, if necessary. A fracture like that could kill a person, if the open wound became infected. Even if it healed, he might limp for the rest of his life. And it was her fault Mr. Dawson had been injured.

After Mr. Higgins left, she ordered a manservant to ride to Whitby to get Dr. Thomas. Then she lay in her bed and stared out the window. She might have just altered the course of a man's life. She had certainly put him out of commission for months, since he could not work behind the counter of a shop with a broken leg. And, to top it all off, he would likely be stuck at Westwinds for weeks while he healed. She had so looked forward to having the house to herself again soon, but it was not to be.

She allowed herself fifteen minutes to wallow in misery over the prospect of her unwanted suitor's extended stay. Then she got to her feet and began making arrangements for Mr. Dawson's invalid care. They would need to hire a servant to tend him, since he had no valet who might have helped with his physical needs. How did one take care of voiding and eliminating if bound to a bed? She wrinkled her nose at the thought. She ought to have asked more questions of Mr. Higgins. She had helped nurse servants through illnesses and injuries before, but not on this scale.

She would need to write to Uncle Elwood, too. She smiled grimly, thinking about how her uncle's matchmaking plans had been overset. Mr. Dawson could hardly beau her about when he was confined to a bed. He would, in fact, be very easy to ignore now. All she had to do was avoid going into his room. That cheered her up a little, encouraging her to get to work. She could not afford to repine all day.

Two days later, Aunt Mary confronted her at breakfast. "My dear, I don't like the way you are treating Mr. Dawson."

"What do you mean?" Emma asked calmly.

She spread butter on her roll and then, knowing it would make her aunt shudder, dunked her roll in her coffee. She could feel Aunt Mary's disgust at that sight, and the corners of her mouth curled up in a smile. She had distracted her aunt. With any luck, Aunt Mary would forget what she was talking about, and—

"That will not work, Emma," her aunt said tartly, dashing all her hopes. This was the problem with living with quick-witted people. They caught on to her tricks. "I will discuss your table manners later. For now, I want to talk to you about poor Mr. Dawson. He is confined to a room with nothing to do. The least you could do is spend some time with him."

Aunt Mary looked steadily at Emma, her green eyes narrowed. She had the same sharp, stubborn chin that Emma had, and she was capable of glaring very fiercely when she wanted to. In a staring contest between the two, Emma was usually the one who looked away. Today was no exception. Emma chalked her aunt's success up to her greater years of experience rather than greater force of will.

"Very well," Emma said. "I will take a book upstairs and read to him. Will that satisfy you?"

"Only if you are polite to him," Aunt Mary clarified. "It is not fair to snub him just because you are angry with your uncle."

"I have not been snubbing him!" Emma grumbled. "I have treated him very politely." She sighed. It would have been far better if she *had* kept ignoring him. If she had never asked him to ride with her, he would not be confined to his bedroom with a broken leg.

Feeling guilty again, she did go upstairs, armed with a book of Felicia Hemans' poetry. Even before she entered his room, she realized the book would not be needed. She could feel waves of feverish pain radiating from the room, and she was not at all surprised to find that Mr. Dawson lay tossing, turning, and burning up.

Emma closed her eyes and said a quick, silent prayer for help. If Mr. Dawson had a fever, that meant his wound had gotten infected despite the magic Dr. Thomas worked to keep out infection. She rummaged in the drawer of the nightstand, looking for the written directions Dr. Thomas had left.

Yes, here was a prescription for a potion the local apothecary could mix up if the wound got infected, along with instructions for cleaning the wound. Aunt Mary had found a manservant to tend Mr. Dawson, but he was nowhere to be seen. How long had Mr. Dawson been left to himself?

Emma brought the prescription downstairs and called for their manservant, Brooks, to ride to the nearest apothecary shop. Then she got a cold compress and a glass of water and went back upstairs. Mr. Dawson seemed to be sleeping, but when she put the compress on his head, he opened his eyes. His feverish state had led him to drop his mental shields, so she could feel the trickle of confusion he felt when he saw her. It was not a flood of emotion. Evidently, he was not one of the people who broadcast his emotions loudly. But she guessed that he had no idea who she was or where he was.

"Mr. Dawson, you have a fever," she told him. "It is a result of your broken leg."

"A fever," he repeated, sounding baffled. "Where am I?"

"You are at Westwinds, near Whitby. I am Miss Ainsworth, your hostess."

49

"At least I have a pretty girl taking care of me," he muttered, and closed his eyes.

Emma frowned, wondering if his fever might be affecting his vision. She did not have a veil on, because she had left off wearing it after the first day of meeting Mr. Dawson. What was the point, when he saw her without it at every meal? Under normal circumstances, she would have accused him of sarcasm or misplaced gallantry, but with his shields down, she could tell he meant what he said quite literally. Well, she thought bitterly, this might be the only time in her life that a good-looking man called her pretty. She might as well savor it.

The potion that Brooks brought back with him from Sleights did not take effect immediately, and Mr. Dawson had a rough night of it. She could feel the waves of delirious panic, fear, and confusion, even from her own bedroom in the west wing. After hours of not being able to sleep, she gave up and put her dressing gown on. Then she walked back to Mr. Dawson's room. She was not at all surprised to see his attendant, Smith, asleep on his cot in the corner, though Mr. Dawson lay muttering in his sleep.

"Don't let him do it," he rasped.

"Don't let who do what?" she asked, thinking he would not understand her in this state. His pitcher of water was empty, and the compress on his head was warm and dry. Emma frowned. Smith must be a terrible attendant.

"Father," he said hoarsely. "Don't let him sign that contract."

Emma drew in a deep breath and hurried away to get the water. She could not help wondering what contract it was, or why the senior Mr. Dawson should not have signed it. Had it something to do with the speculations that had destroyed his family's fortune? She could not ask him that, though. She felt fairly certain Mr. Dawson spoke of something he would not want her to know about.

Chapter Five

June 1814

Henry woke up one morning to find his leg immobilized in a heavy plaster cast, his throat parched, and his face very much in need of a shave. "Water," he croaked, before he even looked to see if there was anyone else in the room.

"Oh, you're awake." He could not place the voice at first. It was a woman's voice, but low for a woman, and sweet. He looked and saw—not a stranger, but Miss Ainsworth, wearing a very pretty lilac morning gown. She had a book in her hand, but she put the book down and got up to pour him a glass of water.

"You ought not be serving me," he rasped. She was a refined young lady and an heiress, not a sick room nurse.

"I am afraid I took the liberty of dismissing your attendant," she said, "since he seemed to be doing such a poor job of caring for you. You have no valet of your own, I take it?"

Henry chuckled ruefully. "A valet?" he repeated derisively. "I would do better to take a position as a valet myself. If I had the fashion sense for it." Unfortunately, that was not the case. He knew how to tie his own cravat, but he tied it in a simple barrel knot rather than attempting any fancy styles.

"We will have to get you one." She reached out to put a wet cloth on his head, but Henry blocked her hand.

"I don't need that," he said irritably. "I need breakfast and a shave." And a visit to the water closet. He looked ruefully at his immobile leg and decided that a bedpan was more likely.

"Dr. Thomas will be glad to hear your appetite is back. He says you must eat more red meat." Again Henry snorted. Miss Ainsworth frowned and gave him what was unmistakably a look of rebuke. "There was a bit of a quarrel between Mr. Higgins and Dr. Thomas. Mr. Higgins bled you, but Dr. Thomas does not believe in bleeding patients. He says you need to eat a hearty diet to make up for the lost blood."

Henry did not know how he was supposed to afford a hearty diet. But as if she read his mind, and perhaps she did, Miss Ainsworth said, "You will be staying here at Westwinds for a couple of months, so—"

"A couple of months?" Henry's voice automatically rose in volume. He cringed at his own loudness.

When he saw Miss Ainsworth visibly flinch, throwing a hand in front of her face, he remembered, too late, that she could feel his emotions if he did not keep his shields up. He slammed them back up and looked away, giving himself time for his irritation to settle.

"It takes time for a bone to heal." She sounded almost hurt. "I know of no magic that can speed that up. And you cannot move until the bone mends."

"I understand that," he said, struggling to keep his voice calm and level, "but can't I heal in my own chambers?"

"Do you have someone to look after you?" She raised her eyebrows. "You will need a servant to tend you."

Henry sighed. "I do not keep a servant." How could a lowly apothecary's assistant afford a servant?

As it was, he sent every spare pound to Mother, who needed it more than he did. He could, of course, go to Scarborough, where his mother shared a house with his grandmother, but if he did that, Mother would fuss over him endlessly. She would also worry about what the family might do without his earnings. No, he preferred not to involve Mother if he could help it. Better that she not know about his injured leg at all.

"Of course," Henry added, "I could probably find a servant temporarily." If he stayed out his month's term, he would have a hundred pounds. That would be enough money to hire a caregiver until his leg healed. "Perhaps I should do that."

"But the journey back to York might injure your leg!" Miss Ainsworth shook her head. "And I don't trust you to take care of yourself properly." Ominously, she settled back down onto the wooden chair near the bed, as if preparing for a long debate on the subject.

"I don't see that it's any of your business whether I take care of myself properly," Henry grumbled. "Anyway, leave me alone so I can piss in peace!" He knew he was being unconscionably vulgar, but his need felt rather urgent. He feared that Miss Ainsworth intended to keep arguing with him instead of leaving him alone.

He expected her to blush and run out of the room, but though her lightly pocked cheeks did flush, her predominant expression seemed one of anger rather than shame. She handed him a chamber pot and left the room, leaving him to figure out how to use it when he could not stand up.

Then, after he filled it, what did he do with it? There wasn't room for it on the bedside table. He lowered it very carefully to the floor, fearing he would spill it. It hurt to move. His whole back ached. Was that a result of his fall from a horse, or the result of lying in bed for so long?

He sat up straight and did some stretches and twists, trying to move his upper body as much as he could without disturbing his injured leg. His pain medication must be wearing off, because even the tiniest movement of the leg made it hurt more. He was in the middle of reaching to touch his toes when Miss Ainsworth returned to the room. She raised her eyebrows but said nothing about his exercises.

"I am going to send our butler in to shave you," she informed him. "He was once my grandfather's valet, though that was many years ago. And then I think you had better have some toast."

His stomach rumbled in response to that suggestion. Toast! He was so very tired of toast. "Weren't you saying I needed hearty meals?" he reminded her.

That had been one of her excuses for keeping him here, right? If he was going to be a prisoner at Westwinds, they had better feed him properly. A steak or chop would be perfect just now. Or perhaps some roast beef and pudding. His mouth started to water just at the thought of it.

"Your stomach needs to adjust to eating regular meals again," she said severely. "We might shock your system if we served you a steak-and-kidney pie right away."

Henry thought a steak-and-kidney pie sounded

perfect. But before he could say that, Miss Ainsworth swept regally out of the room with a faint rustle of her petticoat. Shortly after that, the family's elderly butler entered the room, carrying a straight razor.

Henry sat still while Iverson shaved him, but when the butler finished, he whispered, "I don't suppose you could bring me something more sustaining than toast? We need not tell Miss Ainsworth."

He immediately realized his error. Iverson glared at him and made a sound like, "Humph!" before explicitly stating, "I cannot go against Miss Ainsworth's wishes, sir. She is mistress here. You will eat whatever she asks the cook to send you." He gave Henry a soulful look out of his dark eyes.

"Yes, of course," Henry said, speaking as if he were properly abashed.

In reality, he plotted mutiny. When the housemaid, Hattie, brought in a tray with toast, tea, and a poached egg, he smiled his most winning smile at her. She smiled shyly back, flashing a dimple.

"This looks marvelous, thank you. But if I get hungry, I don't suppose there might be some cold meat in the larder? Or perhaps a slice of pie?" Miss Ainsworth's reference to steak-and-kidney pie had made him crave that.

Hattie's face fell. "I would have to clear that with Miss Ainsworth, sir. She wants you to eat simple, bland foods for now. If you do well with this, maybe you can have toasted cheese for dinner."

She smiled brightly, so Henry tried to smile too, but inwardly he cringed. He had been eating toasted cheese nearly every day for weeks before coming to Westwinds, due to that dentist bill.

If only Mother were better at economizing! She still had the respectable dowry that had been settled on her before her marriage. Although the family were legally prevented from touching the capital of that money, she had access to the income. But raised as the beloved youngest daughter of a wealthy man, then married to a similarly wealthy country gentleman, she had never learned to economize, and now most months she wrote a plea to Henry for funds he did not have.

Henry did not mind supporting his family. Really, he didn't. As the eldest son, that was his duty. But he did wish that Mother would learn to save some of her income for a rainy day so he could keep more of his meager salary to himself. He had grown very tired of toasted cheese.

Even so, he dutifully drank his tea and ate his toast. He had been given butter but no preserves. At least the butter here was of better quality than what he bought in town. He had already noticed that during previous meals, but today, when all he had was toast, butter, and an egg, he felt very grateful for it. Still, he could not help wishing for scones and clotted cream, with jam. If he was not to be allowed meat, could he not at least have something better than toast? The portion was tiny, too. It was as if Miss Ainsworth had forgotten that a large, healthy young man might eat more than a sickly child.

When Hattie returned to take the tray away, he put on his most beseeching face as he asked, "I don't suppose I could have another egg, could I? This is a much smaller breakfast than I am used to."

But Hattie shook her head, keeping her lips tight. "Miss Ainsworth does not want you to eat too much today. Especially not at once. You may have some consommé at midday, if you like."

"That would be lovely," Henry lied.

He sat back in bed and thought wistfully about steak and potatoes. Then he looked around the room for something to do. Hadn't he brought a few books in here before the accident? Yes, they were stacked on the escritoire in the corner. But he could not reach them. He sighed and waited for someone to come and help him. Eventually, he fell asleep. There really was nothing else to do.

He woke at midday, when Hattie brought him the promised bowl of consommé, along with a roll still warm from the oven. He drank the whole bowl in two shakes of a lamb's tail, mopping up what was left with the roll. He did not normally take luncheon, but today he could have eaten a whole plate of sandwiches, or a leftover half-shank of lamb, or a slice of that cold pie Miss Ainsworth had so cruelly taunted him with. Why had she tortured him by mentioning foods he was not allowed to have? And why was she neglecting him for so many hours at a time? Hattie brought him one of his novels, so he at least had something to read, but there were only so many hours a man could spend reading in a day.

A month ago, if someone had told Henry he would have to spend a summer at rest, he would have thought it sounded like a pleasant holiday. In York, he suffered from lack of exercise, not having the time to take the long walks he had been used to when he lived in the country. Standing on his feet in the shop all day was exhausting in its own way. A proper vacation would have been much appreciated.

But now he could not walk or stand at all, and all he had to look at were the four walls of his room. He had thought the wallpaper in this bedroom rather pretty when he first saw it, but by the end of that first day of recovery, he loathed the wallpaper nearly as much as he loathed toast without jam. He would have liked to give Miss Ainsworth a piece of his mind, but she did not set foot in his chamber again that day. He interacted only with the servants, and he knew it would not be right to burden them with his displeasure.

The next morning began the same way. Iverson shaved him and helped him with the bedpan when needed—and if ever there was a humbling moment in his life, Henry thought that must be it. He felt deeply sorry for Iverson, who as a butler ought to have been beyond such tasks.

"I hope Miss Ainsworth finds a valet for me soon," he said apologetically.

"She is interviewing one this morning," Iverson said politely. "If Collins suits, he may be able to take over your care as early as tomorrow."

"Will I get some say in the question of whether he suits?" Henry tried to keep his tone neutral, hoping that he hid the uncertainty he felt. True, he would not be the one paying the valet, but he would like to have some input into the matter all the same.

"That will be for Miss Ainsworth to say."

"Of course it is," Henry said bitterly.

Miss Ainsworth had her way about everything, didn't she? Well, he hoped that power gave her some pleasure. Perhaps that was the real reason she never left Westwinds. Here, she ruled as undisputed queen. In the outside world, though, things would not be so easy. He smirked a little as he imagined how she would fare in a bustling city full of people with more money and power than she had.

Then his bitter smile fell as he looked about the room. He had to reluctantly admit that Miss Ainsworth ran Westwinds well. She had spared no expense in caring for him after his accident, though he had been as much to blame as she had. And he was impressed that she already had a candidate for the role of his valet lined up. He only hoped he would get some say in that man's hiring.

Chapter Six

When Emma walked into Mr. Dawson's room, he was talking to Iverson and, for some reason, had a sour scowl on his face. She frowned as she met his gaze from across the room. When he saw her, he wiped the glower off his face like a child trying to avoid being scolded for a bad attitude.

"Miss Ainsworth," he said politely. "So good to see you today. I hear you may be interviewing a prospective valet this morning?"

"I have already interviewed him," she said, relieved to have good news to report. "Everything seems satisfactory. He will begin work tomorrow morning." She watched as Mr. Dawson lowered his golden brows, a frown marring his face.

"You didn't think that perhaps I would like to meet him before you hired him?" His scowl deepened.

She blinked. That had not occurred to her at all. "I am his employer. And I am mistress here. I am convinced that Collins will do excellently as your valet."

"Thank you for your consideration. I am fortunate to be in such capable hands."

She bit her lip at that. She did not hear sarcasm in his voice, which sounded perfectly polite. She could not read his emotions, because he had his shields up today, for which she was grateful. But she could not help being suspicious. Despite what he said, he did not look thankful.

"Now, I thought that today you might be able to eat something more substantial," she told Mr. Dawson. His whole face brightened, and she watched his Adam's apple move as he swallowed hungrily. "We had a roast chicken for dinner yesterday, and I will have cook serve you some of the cold chicken with a salad on the side for luncheon." Now his face fell. "Is there something wrong with that? Do you not feel that you can handle meat yet?" Perhaps he would do better if kept on a diet of soup for a little longer.

"I feel that I could eat a whole side of beef!" he blurted out. "What I really want is a chop and some potatoes. Didn't the doctor say I needed to eat lots of red meat to make up for being bled?"

She shook her head at once. "I am sure you are not ready for something so heavy. Dr. Thomas is coming this afternoon, and we will ask him then."

She felt certain that Dr. Thomas would support her. When the doctor came, she pulled him aside to discuss her concerns. To her shock and disappointment, he merely chuckled.

"Miss Ainsworth," he said, "have you taken a good look at your patient? He must stand at least six foot two, if not more, and I don't like to guess what he weighed before the accident, but I should think it was at least sixteen stone. He has not eaten properly in days. Let him have a chop and potatoes. If it disagrees with his stomach, he will be the one to suffer, not you. The poor man will have few pleasures while he heals, as it is. Let him eat whatever he has appetite for."

Dr. Thomas did not project his emotions strongly, but he did not shield them tightly, either. Through her empathy, she could tell he was amused by the strict diet she had commanded. In fact, he probably thought she was being a fool.

"Very well, Doctor, since you approve." She forced her stiff lips to smile, as if she appreciated his advice. To be sure, she had no medical degree, merely the experience of nursing sick relatives or servants. In her experience, it could take days for a patient's stomach to recover after a nasty fever like the one Mr. Dawson had. But Dr. Thomas had far more experience than she did.

Emma went downstairs to inform the cook about the change in Mr. Dawson's diet, still quietly fretting over her patient's evident desire to eat himself into an upset stomach. When she came back to the sick room, the doctor pulled her aside to speak to her again. They stood in the hallway, with the door to the bedroom shut, but they both spoke in whispers, as if the patient might overhear.

"Your patient is bored," he said bluntly. "You had better find something for him to do."

"We have brought him books." That was one thing they had plenty of at Westwinds. Mr. Dawson seemed to be a fast reader, so at his request, she had put several novels in a pile on the table next to his bed.

But Dr. Thomas shook his head. "He will need more variety than that. If you ask me, it would be best if he could practice some handcraft, like woodcarving, or basket weaving."

"Basket weaving?" Emma could not quite keep all the surprise out of her voice.

The doctor shrugged. "Just one example. If he would be willing to learn a handcraft like netting, that would do nicely. But he needs something to do."

"I can bring him a pack of cards," Emma said thoughtfully. "And a chess board."

"Yes, if you play chess with him, that would help," Dr. Thomas agreed, "but what would be best of all is if you could find some work for him to do. Have you account books he could balance for you, perhaps? Letters he could write? I should think he would make a good secretary, and that would be work he could do from his bed."

"I will think about that," Emma said doubtfully.

She had never employed a secretary. She balanced the account books and wrote letters herself. She had been doing so since she was seventeen, first with Aunt Mary's assistance, and then on her own. Though of course, since she had not reached the age of majority, Uncle Elwood handled some of the paperwork.

"Perhaps I could let him take over some of my work while he heals." The idea of his involvement in her accounts made her uncomfortable, though. She was used to managing as much as she could herself.

"Cheer up." Dr. Thomas patted her kindly on the shoulder. "Now that he is over his fever, I can work on healing his leg faster. We will likely get him out of here in two months or so."

The contact of his hand on her shoulder conveyed his emotions fairly clearly—he felt sorry for her being stuck with Mr. Dawson so long. The waves of pity she felt made her want to cringe and hide her face.

She did not cringe and she did not so much as look away. She kept meeting the doctor's gaze as she answered, "I am very glad to hear that. And I know Mr. Dawson will be happy to hear it, too."

"Yes, poor man. He is quite unhappy about being

stuck here over the summer. Wanted to know if he could move to Scarborough instead." He shook his head and clucked in dismay. "I cannot advise him to move anywhere until that bone mends. Even with magic, such healing takes time. I will see if I can find a more effective potion for bone healing, though."

"We will do our best to keep him comfortable," Emma promised.

She realized, though, that she had not grasped how difficult that might be. She had imagined Mr. Dawson could entertain himself with books from the library. But now, it seemed, she was expected to find some occupation for him. She nibbled on her thumbnail, trying to think what he could do. Perhaps he would have some ideas of his own. She entered the guest room, still trying to generate ideas.

"Could you at least knock?" Mr. Dawson groused at her. "A man needs his privacy."

Emma nearly opened her mouth to ask what he thought he would do that demanded so much privacy. Then she thought better of it.

"You must be in pain," she said. He was no longer taking laudanum, after all. "Did Dr. Thomas have any recommendations for that?"

"Yes, he prescribed a pain potion that won't knock me out the way laudanum does. One of the servants can fetch it for me. Just as well. I hate the dreams I have when I take laudanum." He shuddered.

She wondered what things he dreamed of, but she could see she ought not ask. Mr. Dawson's amiable politeness had, it seemed, been one of the casualties of his accident. Now, instead of behaving like an overgrown lap dog, he growled and snapped as if she were an intruder he had to chase away. And yet this was Emma's home, not his!

"We will have to find something for you to do." Emma hoped that if she conveyed an attitude of confident cheerfulness, he would snap less.

It did not work as planned. He arched his eyebrows in an exaggerated look of astonishment and said, "Oh, *we* must? Thank you for managing my affairs so well, Miss Ainsworth."

"There is no need to be rude," Emma said sternly. "I am only trying to help." What had happened to her guest? Had the fall from the horse damaged his brain, too? The change in his character really alarmed her. "Dr. Thomas said it would be better if you had some kind of employment."

"Well, he's certainly right about that," Mr. Dawson said. "It would be better if I had kept my job at the apothecary shop and never darkened your doorway. I was a fool to think this would work out well for me." He looked down at his broken leg.

"It hasn't worked out well for me, either," Emma reminded him. "It is not as if I want a patient to tend, you know. We have had to go to a good deal of trouble to care for you."

Leaving aside the issue of doctor's bills and wages for the new valet, Mr. Dawson's injury had upset all her plans. Before the accident, she had thought Mr. Dawson would spend most of his time in the library, leaving her free to happily ignore him, except at mealtimes.

"I am sorry to cause you so much trouble." Mr. Dawson sounded polite now, but once again she thought she saw something about the set of his mouth that suggested he was angry rather than apologetic. "If you would be so kind as to send me to my grandmother's house in Scarborough, I will be out of your hair."

"Dr. Thomas says you are not well enough to travel. We are both going to have to make the best of it." Emma squared her shoulders, intending to circle back to the question of "employment" of some sort for Mr. Dawson. She did not need a secretary, but she had to follow the doctor's orders. "Now, Dr. Thomas says you should have a task to do to keep you occupied. What do you think we could have you do?" Maybe if he kept busy, he would not have the energy to snap at her.

"I am not well enough to work today," he rumbled.

He crossed his arms over his chest and looked away. Because he wore only a light cotton nightshirt, crossing his arms merely demonstrated how muscled he was. What exactly did he do all day in that apothecary shop? Lift hogsheads? Emma forced herself to glance away.

"We will have to talk about that another day," he insisted.

"You are not well enough to work, but you are well enough to ask for chops for dinner?" The words slipped out of her mouth before she realized what she was saying. That did not normally happen to Emma. Usually, she thought through things before she said them. But something about Mr. Dawson prevented her from filtering her words. It was as if he, and he alone, knew how to trigger some hidden engine of impulsiveness in her.

"Eating does not require much cognitive ability," he explained. Emma could hardly argue with that.

"Think about what you might be able to do," she advised. "We will talk more about it later."

She kept thinking about it for the rest of the day. She

thought about it while the Ladies' Aid Society came to gossip and make baby blankets—How many illegitimate children could one parish *have*? She hoped she would at least get to see some of the children when they were born. She loved babies but rarely got to interact with them. Though some of the members of the Society had loud and intrusive feelings, she did her best to pretend she couldn't hear them as she thought about the problem Mr. Dawson presented.

She thought about it again when the cook, Mrs. Seymour, cornered her to discuss a change to the dinner menu that she disapproved of. And she thought about it after dinner, when she sat in the drawing room, mending a torn petticoat while Aunt Mary chatted about some of the gossip they had picked up during the Ladies' Aid visit.

The new curate was said to be courting Mr. Higgins' daughter, and the town was divided as to whether she was likely to accept him. On the one hand, the curate hardly had money enough to support a wife. On the other hand, Mr. Higgins' daughter was said to be ill-tempered, and many in town thought she could do worse.

"To be sure," Aunt Mary said, "they say that Mr. Higgins can give her a nice dowry, and that is sometimes all it takes to attract a good suitor."

"Yes, men are very mercenary when it comes to marriage."

Emma jammed her needle through the hem with more forcefulness than was, strictly speaking, necessary.

"Oh, but my dear, women are no better," Aunt Mary warned her. "When I think of the women who set their caps for your father! All because he was the eldest son and set to inherit. I believe half the reason he liked your mother was that she didn't try so hard to win his favor. Sometimes it's the flower just out of reach that attracts the naturalist's eye." She smiled sentimentally. Emma could tell she felt pleased with her aphorism.

Emma scowled and looked down at her mending. She did not like this subject of conversation, and she did not like the emotions she could pick up from Aunt Mary. Any minute now, her aunt was going to say something about Emma attracting a suitor. She tried to think of a new topic of conversation to introduce. All she could think of was Mr. Dawson, and that subject came perilously close to the question of her finding a marriage partner.

But Aunt Mary needed no prompting to bring up the subject of their injured guest. "My dear, I hope you are being kind to poor Mr. Dawson."

"I will do my best to keep him active and entertained," Emma said. That was not really an answer to her aunt's comment, but she hoped it would satisfy her.

The next morning, she wandered into the library, on a quest for one of the books she had catalogued herself before giving up due to her reaction to the dusty books. She found it where she remembered leaving it: an herbal written by a Yorkshire wizard, Geoffrey Ayles, some two hundred years before she was born. It was in Latin, and she had only a bare minimum of Latin, it not being a language typically taught to girls. But Mr. Dawson had been classically educated, her uncle had said. Time to see just how much of that education he remembered.

She gathered together a few other important accoutrements, including a lap desk that had once belonged to her grandmother, a blank notebook from the study, quill and ink, and of course a Latin-English dictionary. This made a hefty armful, but she managed to carry all of it into the guest room. Her hands being burdened, though, she could not knock. It was all she could do to turn the brass doorhandle to let herself in.

"Does the library come to Dunsinane?" Mr. Dawson exclaimed. "What is all that?"

"Your project," Emma said, and dropped it all on his lap.

Perhaps, in hindsight, she should have used a little more care in putting it down, but she did not believe the high yelp of pain that he uttered. She was sure he embellished his real feelings. He could not be in as much pain as that!

"Good God, woman, didn't anyone tell you how vulnerable men are there? Now that you've lamed me, are you trying to emasculate me, too?"

Emma snorted. She might not have interacted with many human males in the last few years, but she had seen enough of male behavior from bulls, roosters, barn cats, and dogs to believe that male creatures exaggerated the importance of their reproductive function.

"I'm sure you're fine," she told Mr. Dawson. "Pay attention." She ignored the face he made and picked up the herbal. "This is a rare and valuable book, so—"

"I'll try not to spill tea on it," he promised glibly.

"It's worth more than you could earn in five years!" Emma snapped.

He raised his eyebrows. "That doesn't say very much, given how little I earn."

Emma gritted her teeth and looked away to keep from saying something she would later regret. This was difficult, given that she already regretted being here at all. "I only meant to ask you to be careful with it. There are only a few copies in the world, so far as we know. The Ayles family has one at Pennington Hall, and there is one at Oxford, but—"

"Yes, yes, it's a very rare and valuable book," he said testily. "What does it have to do with me?"

"You're going to translate it from Latin into English," she explained. His eyes widened, but for once, he did not argue, so she continued speaking. "Many of these spells are unique to the north of England, and some of them have been lost over time, so translating it will be a great boon to local magicians."

She had hopes that she could induce a publishing house—one of the ones that specialized in spellbooks and magical theory—to publish the translation, for the benefit of historians. And, though she had not told this part to anyone, she secretly hoped that perhaps she could write the introduction to the translation.

"This book is five hundred pages long," Mr. Dawson pointed out. She was relieved to see that he held it carefully, touching only the corners of the pages. "I will not finish this project in two months."

"Probably not," she agreed. "But we can find someone else to finish it. Or you could take it with you to York and finish the translation there." As soon as she said that, she realized how much trust that would place on Mr. Dawson. "That is, if Uncle Elwood likes your translation," she qualified hastily.

"Why doesn't your uncle translate it? Isn't he a wizard?"

"Yes, but he doesn't have the time. His warding spells are much in demand." And, truth be told, Uncle Elwood preferred practicing magic to studying magical history. She was the one in the family with a bent toward history. "But you are a magician too, are you not?"

"Yes, I can work a little sorcery." To demonstrate, Henry snapped his fingers and said "Lux!"

A ball of white witchlight appeared above the open spellbook. Very pretty, and no doubt useful at night. Just now it seemed entirely pointless, since abundant natural sunlight poured in through the window.

He dismissed the light with a wave of his hand. "But this is a book of wizardry, you know." Wizards, unlike sorcerers, used material ingredients in their spells. Their magic worked quite differently.

"I know," Emma admitted. The Ayles family had tended to produce wizards rather than sorcerers, back when they produced magicians at all. There had not been a magician in that family for generations, and from what she heard, the present Lord Colburn, though an Ayles, was as mundane as it was possible to be. "Still, I imagine you would be better at translating it than someone who knew nothing of magic."

"That might be true." He looked down at the book resting open on the lap desk. "I suppose I could do this. I have not used my Latin in years, you know."

"I am sure it will all come back to you." Emma did her best to project confidence. The sour look he gave her suggested he did not appreciate that. "I will leave you to it, then." She swept out of the room, hoping this project would keep him occupied.

Chapter Seven

Uncle Elwood visited Westwinds the Saturday after that, to see how Henry was doing. He brought with him a portable chess set, a box of dominoes, and a board game that Henry had never seen before. "You and Emma can keep each other entertained with these," Uncle Elwood said happily.

Henry shook his head. "I believe your niece expects me to keep myself entertained. I play a lot of Patience when I'm not working." The translation kept him occupied for hours each day, but his hand could only stand so much penmanship before he needed a break.

Uncle Elwood sighed. "I will talk to her. You must remember, she is not used to having a young gentleman about the house."

"So I've noticed." Henry shuddered, thinking of the way she had dropped an enormous pile of books on his lap. If she had grown up with brothers, she would have known better. Probably. "If you talk to Miss Ainsworth, ask her when she's going to let me drink wine again."

"She doesn't let you drink wine?" Uncle Elwood sounded baffled. "She's never been opposed to wine before. She likes a glass of champagne as much anyone." He shook his head and adjusted his spectacles. "Maybe it's just some misunderstanding."

"She seems to think that if I drink, it will bring on a fever," Henry explained. This seemed ridiculous to him.

He had never heard of anyone getting a fever from drinking. A headache? Yes. An upset stomach? Possibly. A fever? Not likely! He had been very sick for a few days, that much was true, but all that ailed him *now* was a broken leg.

"I will speak to her." But Uncle Elwood did something better than talking. As Henry finished his dinner, Uncle Elwood showed up with a decanter of port and a pair of glasses. "I don't care for drinking by myself. Have a drink with me?" Henry would rather it had been cognac, but beggars couldn't be choosers. And port was at least better than claret.

They chatted lightly about local events in York and Whitby, such as the disturbing boom in illegitimate children, the racehorse Lord Brandwyn was said to be preparing for the Doncaster Cup in September, and the state of affairs in France now that Bonaparte was in exile.

"I am so sorry Emma has been rude to you," Uncle Elwood said after his second glass of port. "I don't know what's come over her. She's usually the sweetest girl."

"Are you daft?" Henry shook his head. He had only had one glass of wine, but he had long overcome any reticence whatsoever when it came to talking to Uncle Elwood. "I've figured out the real reason that girl hasn't gotten married."

"Yes?" Uncle Elwood looked hopeful, as if he expected Henry to have some sort of solution for his matchmaking woes.

"She likes being in charge too much," Henry explained.

Uncle Elwood frowned and shook his head. "I don't think you understand our Emma." He poured himself more of the port.

Henry's eyes widened with surprise. He had not remembered Uncle Elwood drinking so heavily during their past after-dinner conversations.

"Emma is very good at managing the household, that much is true," Uncle Elwood conceded. "And she has been used to running the house since she was in her late teens, so she acts older than her years sometimes. But deep inside, she's a very affectionate girl. She gets attached to people, animals, and places. Just watch. She'll get attached to you, and then she won't let you go."

Henry sighed. So that was the new strategy, was it? Uncle Elwood—and probably Aunt Mary—would simply wait for Miss Ainsworth to grow attached to Henry, under the assumption that familiarity would breed affection. And Uncle Elwood still did not seem to grasp the real problem.

"What you're not considering," Henry explained, "is that most men expect to be the master of the house. Miss Ainsworth will not want to marry because she will not want to surrender her authority to someone else."

Henry's father had certainly expected his wishes to be obeyed, no matter what the objection. That had not worked out well for the Dawson family, but no doubt many men operated under the same assumption.

"In the marriage vows, a woman must promise to obey her husband," Henry reminded Uncle Elwood. "I don't see your niece obeying anyone. Do you?"

"Nooo," Uncle Elwood said slowly. "Emma would not want to marry an autocratic man. That much is true. She must find someone good tempered, easy going."

"You mean," Henry said brutally, "she must find a man she can walk over. Very well. But it will be difficult for you to make a match for her, not knowing in advance whether the man you find will be sufficiently submissive for her tastes." Miss Ainsworth would never want to marry *him*, Henry knew, because he did not take her orders quietly.

Uncle Elwood sighed. "I think you are wrong about Emma. But I suppose it is challenging for you to put up with her while your leg heals. I am very sorry for that."

"I do not blame you," Henry said magnanimously. Honesty compelled him to add, "Nor do I blame Miss Ainsworth. It was not her fault the horse bolted."

Though it would have been nice if she had warned him that the beast shied during thunderstorms. If he had been prepared for Bastian to shy, perhaps he could have gotten him under control more quickly. Bastian would not have been injured, and Henry might have gone back to his home sooner, a hundred pounds richer.

"I just wish I did not have to stay here for so long." He looked down into his wine glass, as if it held the solution to his uncomfortable situation.

"Since you are staying for two months rather than one," Uncle Elwood said, "I will double the money I am paying you. What do you say to two hundred pounds?"

Henry nearly spat out his port. Then, overreacting, he swallowed it much too hastily, and almost choked. Uncle Elwood stood up and pounded on Henry's back until he was able to catch his breath.

Henry had to clear his throat before he could speak. "I think that is blood money. You feel guilty for my having broken my leg."

"I feel guilty for taking you away from your chosen career," Uncle Elwood said. "I wish to make up for the time you've lost here at Westwinds. Please say you will accept this reparation?" He looked Henry earnestly in the eyes.

Henry would have loved to refuse the money. He would have loved informing his host that he could not be bought. But if that had been true—if he could really not be bought—he would not have been at Westwinds at all. He was there because he had been willing to sell his body and soul in marriage to Emma Ainsworth, for the good of his family. A man willing to prostitute himself for the rest of his life could hardly claim to be above being paid off after an accident.

"I will accept your money." Henry tried to sound gracious rather than greedy. No doubt most of that money would go to pay bills Mother had no other means of covering. But perhaps a little of it could to go to ensuring that he could afford to visit a chop house now and then for dinner? "But I hope you understand that I have no intention of courting your niece. She and I would not suit."

If Henry and Miss Ainsworth married—an unlikely event, by any rational calculation—they would spend all their time quarrelling. Miss Ainsworth would try to order him around, and she would get short-tempered when he refused to obey. Henry would not expect his wife to blindly obey all his wishes and commands, but he also did not want to have to fight over every single issue. Leave the lovers' spats to barn cats, who were no doubt used to it.

"I understand." Uncle Elwood sounded rather glum. Henry guessed he had still been hoping Henry and Emma would make a match. The older man polished off his port and looked thoughtfully at the decanter but apparently realized he had drunk enough. "I had better go talk to the ladies. I am very sorry you cannot join us, young man."

"I will be fine," Henry said. Though, in fact, it did get quite lonely being left to himself all evening. He would have been glad of the company of one of Emma's kittens, but even they had deserted him, preferring to play outside.

For the three days of Uncle Elwood's visit, Henry at least had company after dinner. The men played cards and talked, sometimes about politics, sometimes about the news of the day, sometimes about magic. Henry was by no means as powerful a magician as Mr. Ainsworth, but he had studied enough to keep up with a theoretical discussion, at least for a little bit. Then Uncle Elwood had to return to his work, and Henry was left without a drinking companion.

But Uncle Elwood must have spoken to his niece about her behavior, because Henry noticed a distinct difference in the way she treated him after her uncle left. She began visiting him every afternoon, sometimes interrupting a nap, and in the evenings after dinner. She offered to play chess and dominoes with him, though it took only one game of *The Mansion of Happiness* to convince them both that it was not worth their time.

At first, Henry took her more pleasant manner to be a passing phase and continued to snap at her, but after a week of the politer, gentler Miss Ainsworth, he relented and returned to his normal gentlemanly behavior. They seemed to have achieved a truce. She let him eat and drink what he wanted, and he ceased snarling when she offered a suggestion about his work.

He began to wonder if he had, after all, misjudged his hostess. Perhaps she really was the sweet, affectionate girl her uncle claimed her to be. Henry would never want to marry her, of course, but that was no reason why they could not be friends.

But their amiable truce ended the day she revealed her plan of seducing her future husband.

Chapter Eight

July 1814

Emma did not set out intending to discuss the matter with Henry Dawson. Their scandalous conversation arose due to his habit of asking impertinent questions. One day while they were playing dominoes, Emma casually mentioned that she did not like touching people. Emotions could be more powerfully conveyed through contact, and sometimes she picked up on undercurrents that might otherwise have escaped her notice. Even if that was not the case, she was much more likely to be overwhelmed by the onslaught of someone else's feelings if she came into physical contact with the person.

"That would be a problem if you were married, wouldn't it?" Mr. Dawson asked. "Fancy reading your husband's mind every time you kissed him!"

"I do not read people's minds!" Emma tried to keep the irritation out of her voice. Mr. Dawson still exasperated her, though not as much as when they first met. "I only sense their emotions and physical sensations. I feel the emotions more strongly and deeply when I touch someone. That is all I meant."

"Even so," Mr. Dawson said. "That would be deuced awkward on your wedding night. I mean, what man would want to go to bed with you, knowing that you would feel everything he felt?"

"What kind of a question is that?" Emma asked indignantly. Well-brought up young ladies did not discuss the marriage bed—except, perhaps, in whispers, when alone with their closest confidantes. Emma had no confidante close enough to talk about this issue, though it was certainly something she had wondered about.

She had once tried to discuss the matter of her empathy and the marriage bed with Aunt Mary. Her aunt, clearly flustered by the question, had gently patted Emma's hand and told her that it would all work out when she was married and that she should not worry about it.

"You and your husband will figure out what to do when the time comes," Aunt Mary had said, sounding wise. Then she had quickly changed the subject to the weather.

Emma had sensed enough discomfort emanating from her aunt to know better than to pursue the topic. She was not brave enough to discuss the matter with Uncle Elwood, and there was no one else to whom she could talk. Until now. Mr. Dawson was neither her friend nor her confidante, but he was a magician, which meant he might understand her dilemma better than most people.

"If you must know," Emma said quietly, "I have long thought that if I became engaged, my fiancé and I would have to experiment before the wedding. To make sure that we would, in fact, be able to engage in marital relations." She blushed as she confessed so unmaidenly a plan.

"Experiment?" Mr. Dawson dropped the domino he had been about to place. He kept his shields as tightly locked as ever, so she could not sense his reaction, but both his voice and his face suggested that he felt horrified. "Do you mean what I think you mean?"

"I mean that we would have to, ah, try things out in advance." Emma's blush grew as she watched his eyes widen. Clearly, it had been a mistake to say anything at all about this plan.

Now Mr. Dawson narrowed his eyes. "Does your uncle know you are planning this?"

"Of course not!" Emma looked out the window, hoping the expression on her face looked nonchalant. But judging from the way her cheeks burned, she suspected she had turned scarlet from embarrassment. "He would be very upset."

"Hmm." Mr. Dawson tapped his fingers on the lap desk that supported their dominoes game. Then a mischievous smile lit up his face. "He certainly will be surprised when I tell him."

"You wouldn't dare!" Emma gasped.

"Don't you think he deserves to know?" Now his smile turned downright wicked. "He is your legal guardian, is he not? I think I have a Christian duty to let him know you are contemplating something so very..." He paused for a moment, as if words failed him, then concluded, "Immoral."

"You, sir, are no gentleman," Emma hissed. She clenched her teeth tightly, feeling her own rage bubbling under the surface like water about to boil over. "To even think of sharing such personal information!"

"You, Miss Ainsworth, are no lady if you are contemplating fornication," he retorted. "And hardly as clever as I took you for, either! You can't have thought this through. What if you became pregnant as a result of your experiments? Worse, what if you caught a disease from your lover?"

"A disease?" Emma repeated, wrinkling her brow. What kind of diseases did you get from lying with a man? The only thing her mind could come up with was fleas or mange, but she was not likely to be going to bed with a man afflicted with those parasites.

"You don't even know to ask him to wear a French letter, do you?" He shook his head in dismay. "I bet you don't even know what that is."

She did not, in fact, have any idea what he was talking about. She kept her mouth shut, not wanting to admit to her ignorance. She clenched her fists tightly, wishing she knew the words to shut her patient up.

But he kept talking. "What if your fiancé jilted you, leaving you ruined? Then you might never marry at all."

"That is a risk I would have to take." Emma decided to ignore all the points she did not understand and concentrate on those things she did comprehend. "Surely you can see that it would be more immoral of me to marry a man if I were not sure I could fulfill my marital duties?" She very much feared that some poor man would be stuck in a marriage in name only because her empathy would not allow her to touch him intimately.

But Mr. Dawson, predictably, did not see it that way. "That would depend on why he married you. If he fancied you, or wanted children, it would be a great disappointment. But if you married a man who only wanted your money, he might not mind. Wealthy men often keep mistresses, don't they? He could satisfy his appetites that way and would not mind the lack of marital duties. That's the sort of man your uncle is likely to find for you, isn't it?"

"How dare you!" Emma had not meant to raise her

voice, but she found herself shouting, much to her surprise.

She gasped and clapped a hand over her mouth, realizing that someone might have heard. She listened, fearing she might hear the sound of footsteps moving down the hall. What if Aunt Mary or one of the maids came to investigate? How would she explain why she was yelling? Worse, what if Mr. Dawson revealed the subject of conversation? But she heard nothing except the sound of her own heartbeat, quickened in anger.

"There is no need for you to take offense. I am merely trying to be practical," Mr. Dawson explained. "It is clear you have no idea what you would be getting into if you carried out this plan. And anyway, I thought you were a devout Christian!"

"It is because I have strict ethics that I refuse to trap a man into a false marriage!" she hissed at him, trying her hardest to keep her voice down. "Besides, I am talking about doing this with my fiancé. In Biblical times, an engagement was more like a marriage. It is not as if I intend to bed some random gentleman the day I meet him!"

"That's a good thing, too," Mr. Dawson grudgingly admitted. "A random stranger would probably not have sufficiently good shields to protect himself from your mindreading. But anyone who could put up with you for more than five minutes would be used to keeping you out of his head. I mean, he would *have* to be good at it, wouldn't he?"

Emma wished, for once, that she was capable of projecting emotions as well as sensing them. She would like to launch a cannonade of fury at Mr. Dawson, who sat there looking smugly confident in his own rightness.

"I suppose you think your shields are good enough to put up with me!" she snapped.

"Well, yes, I do. I mean, it took a broken leg for me to drop them, didn't it? I shouldn't think even the height of passion would be a problem. Not that I have ever tried it."

Emma took this to mean that he had never bedded an empath. The other possible interpretation—that he had never bedded a woman at all—seemed extremely unlikely to her. So good-looking and personable a young man must find it easy to find partners among the lower orders of women. He certainly sounded as if he knew what he was talking about, whereas Emma felt that every word she uttered underscored her ignorance.

"Too bad you can't test it," Emma said. He looked at her blankly. "Because of your broken leg, I mean."

To her surprise, he laughed at her. "My leg may be broken, but all my other body parts work perfectly well!"

"But…" Emma floundered, not sure how to articulate her objection. "I do not see how you could get in the right position."

The only reproductive acts she had seen in person had been acts of animals, but there were some rather disturbing erotic prints in her grandfather's library. She preferred not to think of them if she could help it, but she did not remember seeing any that involved a man flat on his back. Wasn't it always the woman on the bottom? Her face began to burn with embarrassment again. Really, this was a most improper conversation.

And to crown her humiliation, her objection just made Mr. Dawson laugh harder. "Much you know about it! Haven't you ever heard of riding St. George?" Emma had not, and her face must have shown it, because he clarified. "For your information, it is perfectly possible to do it with the woman on top." Then he sighed. "I ought not be telling you these things." He no longer sounded amused. "Your uncle would be very unhappy if he knew I was corrupting you."

"Are you sure?" Emma asked, thinking about her uncle's possible motives in selecting Mr. Dawson. "He must have chosen you because you were good at shielding your mind. Perhaps he thought ahead to what we would do in bed if we were married."

Once again, she had spoken without considering the impact of her words. Their eyes met across the room, and a shiver crawled down her back. If she were superstitious, she would have said it was an omen, like someone walking over her grave. Mr. Dawson said nothing, but a flush rose on his cheeks and he turned his head away, so she thought she could take a guess at what he was thinking, too.

Really, she did not understand how they had gotten into a conversation so wildly inappropriate. And now their talk had put outrageous and disturbing ideas in her head. That must be why young ladies were not supposed to discuss these matters. Someone should have warned her how dangerous it was!

"I think I hear my aunt calling me," Emma lied. She used the brightest, most cheerful voice she could command, and tried to ignore the way her cheeks burned from that telltale blush. "I had better go."

"Yes, quite." Mr. Dawson looked out the window as if there were something particularly fascinating to be seen from it—though that window looked out into the barnyard, so that was unlikely. Also, his face remained bright red. "I will see you later."

Emma prevented herself from bolting, as much as she wanted to do so. She walked with her back straight as an arrow, and her chin lifted high, as if she had nothing to be ashamed of. As if she talked with handsome young men every day about going to bed.

But once his door shut behind her, she bolted for her room and locked her own door as soon as it closed. Even that did not make the room feel private enough. For a brief, childish moment, she contemplated hiding in the wardrobe or under the bed, as if she could escape her humiliation that way. She could not remember ever feeling so ashamed of herself. What had she been thinking?

Worse, what was she thinking *now*? The idea that had popped into her head was ridiculous, unbelievable, and immoral. She did not want to go to bed with Henry Dawson! She barely liked him, and she certainly did not love him. They were not married, nor engaged, nor would they ever be. It would be wrong, very wrong, to make him the subject of her experiments. Even if, in some ways, he was the ideal subject.

In truth, men like Mr. Dawson did not often come her way—and Emma did not mean that in regard to his rare good looks. Exceptional as he might be as a physical specimen of manhood, his magical abilities were more important. Emma had met few people who were as good at shielding their minds from her as Mr. Dawson, which meant there would be a greater chance of success with him than with most other men. When else was she likely to find a man like that? Or, if having found him, how likely was it that such a man would be a house guest in her home, making him accessible for …experimentation?

And no one thought she needed a chaperone when she was with Mr. Dawson, because he was injured. Indeed, both her aunt and uncle had practically begged Emma to spend hours alone in a room with Mr. Dawson, which would under normal circumstances have been forbidden. Marriageable young ladies and young gentlemen were not normally allowed to converse alone that way. And now she knew why. Truly, chaperones were necessary!

Emma and Mr. Dawson had been in the habit of closing the door, since it would otherwise slam shut from the draft, so no one would think twice if they saw the door to his room closed. Therefore, it would be easy enough to close and lock the door one evening, or one afternoon. If they pulled the curtains closed, no one would be able to see in from the barnyard. And then they could do whatever they wanted to do, so long as they were not too loud.

Not that Emma wanted to do anything with him! Of course not. Perhaps this was the prompting of the Devil. Emma had never experienced such a thing and was not really sure she believed such things happened, but she had trouble explaining in any other way the thought that haunted her mind.

True, when she was younger, she'd had fantasies about meeting a sweet, kind, gentle man who would not mind about the pockmarks on her face, who would love her for who she was. She had given up on those fantasies by the time she turned eighteen, because she had learned by then that, as an heiress, she would always be viewed by potential suitors as a source of financial gain.

If Emma had been a character in a fairy tale, she could disguise herself as a beggar woman and go in quest of a knight, loyal and true, who would love her apart from her fortune. But life was not a fairy tale. And Henry Dawson was not a knight errant. Nor was he a sweet, kind, gentle man. He was sharp-tongued and blunt and said ridiculous things that a gentleman should not say. It must be his fault she was indulging in depraved thinking, such as trying to picture how a woman could be on top in amorous congress.

And, she reminded herself, he was a fortune hunter, to boot. He had come to Westwinds intending to court her, all because he wanted to be rich again. He would have willingly married her, yes, but only so he could use her inheritance to return to the role of country squire that would have been his if not for his father's speculations.

Moreover, thanks to his too-loose tongue, she knew he would not have intended to be a faithful husband. If he had married her, he would have kept a mistress for his "appetites" (using Emma's money!) and might not even have been willing to give her children. It was, she reminded herself, very good that she had learned that about him. Only think what would have happened if she had been foolish enough to let him woo her!

If she had been a weak, sentimental girl, she might have fallen for the charm he had initially displayed. Emma was only human, after all, and she could not deny that Mr. Dawson was, so far as personal appearance went, one of the best-looking men she had ever seen. It was fortunate indeed that she had been on her guard against him from the start. Otherwise, who knew what might have happened? A good-looking man who would do anything for money could be quite dangerous.

Emma told herself all these things. But she could not stop wondering if it were true that he would do *anything* for money. The more she thought about it, the more she wondered if she ought to put him to use, since his injury confined him to Westwinds. The question was, how much must she offer to get him to do as she wanted?

Chapter Nine

Henry did not feel quite as ashamed after that conversation as Emma did, but he felt embarrassed, regretful, and also hot and bothered. He knew perfectly well that he had said things to Miss Ainsworth that a gentleman should never say to a single young lady. But she had provoked him!

He still felt astounded by her audacious plan to "experiment" before marriage. To be sure, that was none of his business...except that she pointedly reminded him that if he had succeeded in the task Mr. Ainsworth had assigned him, it *would* have been his business. He would have been the man bedding her.

And now he could not get that vision out of his mind. He was most definitely not in love with Emma Ainsworth, but he would have enjoyed bedding her. Who wouldn't? Even the loose lines of her high-waisted dresses could not entirely hide the fact that she had delightfully rounded hips, and as for her bust, well, one could hardly fail to notice that she looked well in low-cut evening dresses.

Henry knew the form hidden by the many layers of clothing women always wore must be downright beautiful. And if Uncle Elwood's plan had worked, he might have had the right to disrobe her. He sighed, for the first time truly regretting that he and Miss Ainsworth had not hit it off well.

He had never understood why she insisted on hiding her face from strangers. Who cared about a few pockmarks when she had such a saucy, bewitching mouth? Anyone could be forgiven for wanting to kiss that mouth. He had not realized how appealing it was until now, when he took the time to imagine…things he ought not to be imagining. Now he wished he could empty a bucket of water on himself to cool off. Better yet, a cold, spring-fed mountain lake would be perfect right now. He could plunge in, and his body, at least, might forget about Miss Ainsworth, whatever his imagination might do.

Not surprisingly, his dreams that night were all about women—or rather, about one particular woman. He woke up with a start and wondered, for the first time, if his mental shields stayed up when he slept. Could Miss Ainsworth feel emotions from dreaming people? If so, did that mean she knew how randy he felt? He prayed that her empathy worked only on waking minds.

Miss Ainsworth avoided him all that afternoon. This annoyed Henry, because he had an apologetic speech prepared for her, and he anxiously waited to give it to her. But she did not come to his room until well after dinner. He had, in fact, given up hope of seeing her that day, and he had already had Collins bring him his toothbrush and the washing basin so he could get ready for bed. He was just about to adjust the pillows so he could go to sleep when he heard the knock at the door.

"You may come in," he said, half-thinking it might be Collins come back to ask him some last question about the morning.

Collins had been trying to convince Henry that though he was bedbound, he should still dress in a waistcoat and cravat, at least, rather than wearing nothing but a shirt every day. Henry thought this was stupid, given that he could not leave the room. Who did he have to impress?

But the knock at the door was not from Collins. Instead, Miss Ainsworth entered the room, still wearing her evening dress. Today it was that silk dress in a seductive shade of red that did wonders for her dark hair and dark eyes. Henry gulped and averted his eyes.

Damn her and her immodest conversation! Now he could not look at her without thinking about taking her to bed. And he still had more than a month of recuperation time, didn't he? That meant a month of torture, unless he came up with some way of distracting himself.

Also, he found himself wondering if perhaps Collins was right. Maybe he should start dressing again, even if he could not get out of bed. He must look terrible, wearing just a plain shirt day after day.

Henry cleared his throat. "I am glad to see you again, Miss Ainsworth. There is something I wanted to say to you."

"Good." She approached the chair beside the bed slowly, averting her eyes from his face. She must feel ashamed of their earlier conversation, of the things she had admitted and the even worse things he had said to her—had he really discussed sexual positions with her? "There is something I wish to say, too. But you may go first."

Now Henry tried to look her in the eyes, but she kept looking down at her folded hands. She bit her lip and, God help him, he wondered what it would feel like if she bit *his* lip. Not a hard bite, just a little nibble.

"You had something to say?" she prompted.

"Oh, yes." Henry's voice did not sound right at all. He cleared his throat and tried again. "I merely wanted to apologize for my words yesterday. They were not at all proper. I don't know what came over me. I should never have said such things to a respectable young lady. Your uncle would be rightfully furious with me if he knew." He very much hoped Uncle Elwood would never know about that conversation.

"Ah, please, pay it no mind," she said hurriedly. But a hint of a blush rose on her cheeks. "That is not exactly what I wanted to talk about, though." She looked back down at her hands.

"No?" he prompted, when she remained quiet for entirely too long.

"I have a deal to propose to you." He watched, puzzled, as her face grew redder and redder. Normally, he thought she had a charming blush, but now she rather resembled a tomato.

"A deal?" Henry used the softest, gentlest voice he could muster, seeing that she felt very uncomfortable with the conversation. He could imagine no deal she could want to make with him. She did not like him, after all.

"Yes." She looked up and nodded her head. Then she squared her shoulders bravely and met his eyes. "You see, I think you were right, yesterday, when you said you would be able to keep your mental shields up even in the middle of, er, a passionate moment. Which," she gulped, "makes you an ideal subject for experimentation."

"Subject for experimentation?" He puzzled over that for a moment. When a suspicion arose in his mind, he told himself she could not mean what he thought she meant. She could not mean the experimentation she had discussed with him yesterday. She had said she would do that only with her fiancé.

"Yes." She looked away, as if fascinated by the wallpaper. "I am willing to recompense you for your time and effort, of course."

"You... What now?"

"I will pay you five hundred pounds if you would be so willing as, to, um, deflower me."

It took Henry a moment to get over his shock. "Are you mad?" he hissed. "You can't go around offering proposals like that to strange men!" That was only the tip of the iceberg when it came to his objections, but it seemed like the most important point.

"You aren't a stranger! We have known each other for more than a month now. Nearly two months! Besides, you were hand-picked for me by my uncle. If he thought you good to enough to marry me, you must be good enough to, ah, bed me."

"I am not your husband," Henry said sharply. "Nor am I your fiancé. I thought you said you were going to experiment with your fiancé? You had some nonsense to support your idea—"

"It wasn't nonsense!" Now she turned to look at him, her eyes flashing. "But I've thought better of that idea. Wouldn't it be nearly as bad to wait until engagement to find out that...things...wouldn't work? I mean, there would be so much heartbreak. What if the gentleman insisted on marrying me anyway? That could be for the happiness of neither of us. But I could hardly go to bed with a man while he was courting me. He would think I was wanton."

"But throwing yourself at me isn't wanton?" Henry could not follow her logic at all, and he did not know if that was because there was no logic, or if it was because he was in a state of shock.

"No one would ever know!"

Henry raised his eyebrows at her.

She wilted a little. "I mean, yes, I would have to tell my husband, if I married. But if things didn't work with you, I would know they wouldn't work with anyone, since no one is likely to have stronger shields than you do. So this would be a sort of…litmus test? To help me figure out whether I should just stay single."

Henry could see so many problems with this plan that he did not know where to begin. "But what, exactly, would you tell your husband when you married? 'Oh, by the way, I had a fling with a young man, and I lost my virginity to him, but don't worry, I never loved him the way I love you!'?"

"I would tell him the truth!" Miss Ainsworth snapped. "Anyone who married me would know about my empathy, and about the problems it causes."

Henry shook his head. "And do you think a gentleman would want to marry you after that revelation? Men of your class expect their brides to come to marriage as pure as the wind-driven snow."

Miss Ainsworth crossed her arms in front of her chest and pouted. "A man who really loved me would not mind."

"Or a man who really needed the money," Henry suggested. Money made the world go round, after all. There were probably men who would be willing to overlook a whole string of affairs if it meant living a life of luxury.

"Yes," Miss Ainsworth snapped, "you've already made it very clear that you think the only reason a man would marry me is for my fortune. No need to remind me of that."

"What? No, you misunderstand me." Henry lifted his hands up in a placating gesture. He did not have to be an empath to see that his words had upset Miss Ainsworth. "I just meant that's how your uncle seems to be trying to sell you."

"Sell me?" She gave him a wide-eyed stare.

Damn, he was just digging the hole deeper. "No, no," Henry said, "I meant the other way around. The whole point of his matchmaking scheme is that he's trying to find a man who will sell himself in exchange for access to your fortune. You're not the one being bought. Your husband is."

That is, if she ever found a husband who would suit her. He had real doubts about that. He had no idea what kind of suitor she was looking for, but he would wager that she would be hard to please.

"As if that's any better!" she protested.

"It's better than what you're proposing to me!" This had been bothering Henry for some time, but he had put his anger aside to talk about more important matters. "What made you think I would be your fancy man?" It was the most insulting offer anyone had ever made to him.

Her jaw dropped, and she clasped her hands together. "But you were perfectly willing to marry me for my money. What makes this different?"

"It is entirely different!" Henry crossed his arms across his chest and jutted his chin out a little. "I do not sell my favors."

"How is it different?" she persisted, lowering her brows. Her face no longer looked kissable. On the contrary, she looked like a dog about to bite. If she had lifted her lip to show her teeth, he would not have been surprised. Henry supposed he ought to be grateful for this argument. If nothing else, it had driven all his amorous fantasies out of his head. He had rather box with Miss Ainsworth than tup her just now.

"Isn't it obvious?" Henry said.

"No. Explain to me as if I were stupid." She arched her eyebrows and smirked at him. Henry opened his mouth to answer her, then paused. Why was his brain failing him now? There must be many ways in which prostitution differed from marrying for money. Right?

"For one thing," Henry said, stalling for time, "marriage is a holy ordinance of the church." He felt grateful for his mother's attention to his religious education. It supplied him with the tools of battle just now. "Whereas fornication is a sin. In fact," he said, warming up to this argument, "lust is one of the seven deadly sins."

"But traditionally, the sins of the flesh were considered less important than the spiritual sins, such as pride. Lust is the least serious of the seven deadly sins." She smiled rather smugly, as if pleased with her own reasoning.

"Tell that to all the mothers who keep their daughters away from French novels," Henry grumbled. "And how do you know that, anyway?"

"I read," she said succinctly. "You should try it sometime."

Henry glanced at the pile of books next to his bed and thought wistfully of how pleasing it would be to launch one at Miss Ainsworth. Not that he would ever throw a book at anyone, and certainly not at a woman.

"If selling one's body for pleasure is wrong, then it must be wrong for people to marry for money. And you, sir, came here with the very purpose of marrying me purely for my fortune, did you not?"

"No, that's not the same!" Inwardly, Henry cursed himself, knowing that he was losing the argument. And she knew it too, damn it! The smile on her face grew even more smug.

"If you had married me," she continued, "It would be your duty to consummate the marriage, would it not? And you would owe me a debt. The marriage debt."

"What are you even talking about? Where did you get that phrase?" Henry knew he was staring at her incredulously, but he could not help it. He had never heard of "the marriage debt."

"From *The Introduction to the Devout Life*," she said blithely. "I told you, you should read a book."

"I only read books by Protestant theologians," Henry said scornfully. Drawing ammunition for debate from Papists was cheating!

"Anyway, in medieval religion, people believed that husbands and wives owed each other a debt and that it was wrong to refuse each other."

"Refuse each other what?" Henry knew perfectly well what she meant, but he suspected it would embarrass her to have to spell it out. And he was right.

Miss Ainsworth blushed again and looked down at her hands as she answered. "Refuse each other marital relations! Never mind that. The point is, if you married me…you would have to, you know." Henry smirked as her blush deepened. He stared at her with his best imitation of a look of stupidity until she blurted out, "You would have had to lie with me."

"But I'm not married to you," he pointed out. "So I can't do that."

The whole argument had gone in some enormous circle, and they were right back where they had started. But Miss Ainsworth looked more flustered than before, which might be an advantage. Maybe he had the upper hand after all.

"That's not the point!" She sounded distinctly irritated. "My point is that if you had married me for money, you would have owed me, um, relations as a result of that bargain." Henry tensed up, suddenly realizing where she was going with this line of argument. "So you have no right to act so indignant if I offer you money to have relations with me now," she continued.

She lifted her chin boldly and stared him in the eyes. "You would have been as much my fancy man if you had agreed to marry me for my fortune. And you were willing to do that. Stop acting as if I've offended you! I am only asking you to do something you would have done anyway."

"But I didn't agree to marry you!" Henry wondered how he was going to get out of this trap.

"You know perfectly well that you came here for the purpose of courting me. Didn't you?"

"Yes, I suppose so." Henry dropped his eyes.

He could have lied about that, but he saw no point to lying. They both knew it was true. He had come here with the intention of wooing and marrying Miss Ainsworth, and he had been willing to do that because he wanted to restore his family's fortune. Marrying an heiress was the only chance he saw of doing that.

"So you did intend to marry me." He glanced up and saw the smirk had returned to her face.

"I considered it," Henry said warily. "I never actually committed to it. You'll notice that I never proposed." Because it had taken him only two days to realize his courtship could not prosper. Miss Ainsworth had made it very clear that she did not want to be wooed by him.

"Look, this is all beside the point," he continued. This argument maddened him. He wanted to bury his head under a pillow and forget it had ever happened. "I am not engaged to you, I am not married to you, and I will not sell my virtue. You will have to find someone else to experiment on. The only woman I am planning on bedding is my wife. You don't want to marry me, do you? Then this conversation is over."

Miss Ainsworth narrowed her eyes. She lifted one arm so she could rest her chin on her hand as she looked at Henry. Henry grew nervous. He could not imagine what she was going to try next, but from the look on her face, she was not ready to throw down her arms. He felt even more certain of that when a slow smile crossed her bewitching lips. Something about that smile made the hairs on his arms stand up straight.

"Very well, Mr. Dawson," she said. "You win."

Henry blinked. If he had won, why was she smiling like the proverbial cat who had stolen the cream? "What have I won?" he asked cautiously.

"My hand in marriage, of course," she replied. "I accept your proposal. We are betrothed now."

Chapter Ten

Emma knew she was grinning like a fool, but she could not stop. She had him trapped, and he must know it. Or, if he did not know it, he would soon, once she spelled it all out for him. Mr. Dawson did seem to need to have things explained to him in more detail than she would have thought necessary for a man who had gone to Cambridge. Even if he had left before earning his degree.

Mr. Dawson had frequently looked flummoxed throughout this conversation, but the blank stare he gave her now might win the award for most stupefaction. "I never made you a proposal!"

"Yes, you did," Emma said. "Just now you said, 'You don't want to marry me, do you?' You did not wait for my answer to your question because you assumed you knew the answer. But I am telling you now that I *do* want to marry you. I accept your proposal. We are betrothed. And," she continued, feeling a sense of victory that welled up inside her and flooded her veins, "If you try to back out of our engagement, I can sue you for breach of promise." She knew perfectly well he did not have the money to pay any kind of damages. He would have to do as she asked.

Mr. Dawson rested his head on one hand and sighed. "Is there anything I can do to get you to leave me alone?"

"Marry me," she suggested.

The second the words were out of her mouth, she found herself questioning them. When had that become the goal? She was only trying to get Mr. Dawson to let her experiment on him. Her triumphant smile began to falter as she realized she might have gotten herself into a predicament she had not anticipated.

"You want me to marry you?" He raised his eyebrows. "I thought you just wanted me to tup you."

"One implies the other." She tried to keep her voice cool, calm, and collected, though his use of the vulgar word rattled her a little. Why couldn't he speak more decorously? "As we discussed yesterday, I feel it incumbent on me to…to…"

"To experiment with your fiancé?" he suggested drily. "Is that what this is about? You will say we are engaged so that I will do what you want, and then you will jilt me once you've stolen my virtue?" He shook his head.

"What virtue?" she protested. "You're a man. No one cares about men's virtue." Everyone expected young men to be unchaste, at least wealthy young men. Only women had to wait for marriage.

"I care!" he protested. "And so would my wife! In the unlikely event that I ever marry, that is." He frowned at that thought. "It is not as if I can afford to marry, anyway."

"But it's not as if you're a virgin," she argued.

He looked at her. She stared back. She expected him to back down or argue, but he did not. He merely raised his eyebrows again.

"Do you mean to say that you've never bedded a woman?" She could not believe it. But he nodded his head.

She sat still, shocked into silence. Then she got angry. Yesterday he had made her feel like a fool for all the things she did not know. He had laughed in her face, as if he were an expert on the subject! Today, she found out he was just as inexperienced as she was. That was not fair.

"Since I am going to be your wife," she said, biting each word off angrily, "I can assure you I will not be upset at you for…letting me take your virtue." Could a woman do that? What did that even mean? How could virtue be *taken*? Emma decided she ought to stop talking like a character in a Richardson novel.

"Let us be clear here," Mr. Dawson said crisply. "You do plan on jilting me, don't you? You aren't really going to marry me?"

Emma's stomach churned. How had she gotten into this situation? How had she strayed from her goal? Her plan had been to experiment with Mr. Dawson so that she knew whether there was any point in even trying to find a marriage partner. She had never intended to *marry* Mr. Dawson.

Mr. Dawson might be the handsomest man she had ever seen, but the two of them would not suit. Living with him would probably mean a constant storm of verbal battles. That might be intellectually stimulating, true, but it could hardly be conducive to marital harmony. She wanted a sweet, kind, gentle husband who loved her. Mr. Dawson would never be that.

"I'm right," Mr. Dawson concluded, once it was clear that Emma could not come up with an answer. "No, thank you. You cannot use me and toss me aside like that. I am not your plaything."

Emma gulped. She could see one solution, but it was

more dangerous for her than for him. "What if I promise not to jilt you?"

"Promise not to jilt me? You mean you would actually marry me?" Incredulity was written all over his face.

Emma swallowed again. "Yes. If that is what you still want when the engagement is over, I will marry you." She would just have to make certain he did not want that. But that should be easy. Mr. Dawson did not like her. He would not really want to spend his life in the same household with her. He could not be *that* greedy for her fortune. Could he?

Mr. Dawson sighed. "Look, Miss Ainsworth, I don't think either of us are thinking very clearly. I recommend you go to bed. When you wake up in the morning, you will realize this is not what you want. And I assure you, I will hold no grudges. I will happily release you from whatever promise you think you have made. But I do not want to speak any more of this tonight. I have the headache, and I wish to be left alone."

"And what if I wake up and realize I do want this?" she asked softly.

He rumpled his hair, twisting his mouth at a bitter angle. "If you insist on holding me to a proposal I never meant to make, so be it. I am not the man to jilt a hopeful bride. And if I marry you, I will do my best to be a good husband to you." He glared at her. "More than that I will not promise."

"Very well," she said. "I will see you in the morning." She made it outside the room and then leaned against the wall of the corridor, feeling her legs were too weak to carry her farther.

How had her game gotten so out of hand? She could

not tell if she was winning or losing. She slowly sank to the floor and buried her face in her folded arms. For some reason, one that even she could not explain, she did not want to concede this fight. There had to be a way to win. She just had not thought of it yet.

What she was asking for did not seem like a hardship for Mr. Dawson. On the contrary, she was under the impression that most men enjoyed bedding women. A chill settled in her stomach as she considered the possibility that he was so revolted by her appearance that he did not want to lie with her. He had never implied such a thing, but perhaps he felt that would be too terrible to say. She swallowed, trying both to clear the lump from her throat and to stuff that thought back into the deepest recesses of her mind. If that was the case, he could close his eyes and imagine someone else.

As for his objection about his future wife minding his unchastity, she did not think it held water. First, because no one expected the same purity from a man that they did from a woman. Perhaps clergymen were expected to be chaste, but other gentlemen? No, only a very high stickler indeed would take offense at a young man having lost his virginity before marriage.

Second, because he himself had admitted he was unlikely to marry, given his unfortunate financial situation. If he never married, there was no future wife to wrong. And thirdly, because she would hold up her end of the bargain and marry him after all if that was what he really wanted. She prided herself on being a woman of her word.

The only one of his objections that stood up to scrutiny was his claim that he did not want to be used as an object. That, she had to admit, had some truth to it.

But again, there was the fact that he had been willing to court her for her fortune. He could not claim to have a high sense of self-worth if he had been willing to marry for money.

So he ought not refuse her this. Especially since they were, in fact, engaged. He had as much as admitted that. He had said he would marry her if she wanted. Now all she had to do was remind him of all the reasons why it would be better for them not to wait until after the wedding to find out how things might work for them.

Emma hauled herself to her feet, still leaning on the wall for support. Then she went back to her room and put herself to bed as she always did. She went through the routine of brushing her teeth and washing her face, letting down her hair and combing it out.

As she stood in front of the mirror, she felt the first jolt of uneasiness. What exactly was she trying to do with Mr. Dawson? She did not want to marry him, so why had she tricked him into an engagement? Anyone would think she was trying to play the courtship game her uncle wanted her to play.

But she did not want an arranged marriage. She had never wanted that. To be loved might be very sweet, but she could not stomach the idea of a man marrying her for the sake of financial security. That being the case, she did not understand how her plan had gotten so out of hand. She hoped the morning would bring some clarity about what to do next.

Sure enough, she woke in the morning, looked out the window at the gently falling rain, and knew what she needed to do. She owed Mr. Dawson an apology. It had been wrong, very wrong of her to try to seduce a virtuous young gentleman. She could hardly believe she had been so brazen as to propose that they corrupt one another. Her stomach churned as she thought about it now, in the light of the day. What must Mr. Dawson think of her? Worse, what if he told her uncle about her unmaidenly behavior?

Emma sat hunched up in bed, her arms wrapped around her knees as she listened to the distant sound of rain. Her room was warm, snug, and comfortable. As she looked around, it occurred to her for the first time that though she had left the nursery years ago, her bedroom still looked like a child's room. Indeed, her dollhouse still stood in one corner of the room! Many of her books from childhood still sat in the bookcase, though they were joined by a growing collection of novels and works of devotion.

A border of pink roses ran across the top of the wallpaper, and the bedclothes were a matching shade of soft rose. It was a pretty color, but was it not, perhaps, a little juvenile? Emma wondered if she had been behaving like a child, too.

Reluctantly she climbed out of bed. She rang for Hattie to help her dress, though she usually dressed herself. Today she did not seem to have her normal morning energy. Hattie even remarked on it, asking if she felt sick. Emma shook her head. She did not feel sick. She felt foolish. She was ashamed to face Mr. Dawson again, but she had better visit him after breakfast to make her apologies.

At breakfast, she noticed that Aunt Mary seemed nervous about something. Her aunt spilled the cream when she passed it to Emma, and she chipped her saucer putting her teacup down.

"Oh, dear," Aunt Mary said. "Such a shame. I do

love this pattern. Your mother picked it when she married, you know. It was a gift from our parents."

"Yes, I know," Emma said patiently. "Do not worry, Aunt Mary. We have more saucers." And it was a tiny chip. The saucer could still be used when only the family were breakfasting.

"Hattie," Aunt Mary said, "Please go and check that there are no leaks in the third story. We cannot have water getting into the house."

Hattie's eyes widened, but she bobbed her head and said, "Yes, Miss Barker."

Emma stared at her aunt, wondering what on earth she was thinking. The roof had been repaired last summer. There were no leaks now. And if there were, someone would notice soon enough. The third story was where the servants' bedrooms were located. Someone there would certainly complain if water got in a bedroom.

"I wished to speak with you privately," Aunt Mary whispered. "My dear, I don't want to alarm you, but Iverson told me this morning that one of the housemaids saw you leaving Mr. Dawson's room very late last night. She said that the door had been closed, and that you must have been there for hours!"

Emma gulped. She felt the teacup in her hand begin to shake, so she put it down hastily. Luckily, she did not chip the Blue Willow saucer.

"Of course, I visited him." She kept her voice pleasant and light, as if she discussed nothing of any importance. "You and Uncle Elwood have begged me to keep him entertained. You have nothing to fear, Aunt Mary." She hoped her smile did not look as tremulous as it felt. "It is not as if Mr. Dawson could offer me any sort of injury. He is confined to a bed." Her face heated up as she thought about what she had proposed he do with her on that bed.

"Yes, I know, dear." Aunt Mary gave her a reassuring smile. But she still spoke in an anxious whisper. "But it does not look good, you know. Perhaps we were wrong to encourage you. We never meant for you to stay in his room until the wee hours of the morning! People do gossip, Emma. If the maid felt bold enough about it to tell Iverson, she likely told others in the household. And our servants may gossip with people outside the household. I worry that you may already have damaged your reputation. And who knows whether Mr. Dawson will take responsibility?"

"Oh, you need not worry about that, Aunt Mary," Emma said earnestly. She could not bear to see her sweet, kind aunt so distressed by her behavior. Even if she had not, as of yet, actually done anything immoral with Mr. Dawson. "Mr. Dawson's intentions are honorable."

Mr. Dawson certainly had no desire to seduce her. He had made that abundantly clear. What she did not add was that his intention was to run away from her as soon as he could, and never see her again. Still, that was an honorable intention, wasn't it?

Aunt Mary had been looking down into her teacup, but now she lifted her eyes to stare at Emma. "Has he declared himself?" she asked, her voice tense. "That would be the best thing that could happen, under the circumstances. The gossip will die down eventually if he does the right thing. But surely you aren't engaged?"

Anxiety, tinged with a touch of hope, rolled off her. Aunt Mary very much hoped that Emma and Mr.

Dawson were engaged. The doubtful, wistful tone in her aunt's voice went straight to Emma's heart, while her aunt's unshielded emotions played havoc with her sense of reason.

"He has declared himself," Emma said, giving her aunt a reassuring smile, "and I accepted him. We are betrothed. So you have nothing to worry about, Aunt Mary."

Chapter Eleven

Henry hated being shaved. Frankly, he preferred to do it himself, but the truth was that he could not do as neat and quick a job as his valet could. So he let Collins shave him, though it always made him nervous to give someone else so much control over him. It was not so bad when his chin was being shaved, but he inwardly cringed whenever the razor came near his throat. Today the memory of last night's conversation with Miss Ainsworth distracted him, and he jumped a little at the touch of the razor.

"Did I cut you, sir?" Collins asked anxiously. "I don't see any blood."

"No, no. Just something I was thinking of."

Henry closed his eyes and thought calming thoughts, listing all the things he loved about life. The first violets of spring. The scent of roses in June. The smell of a stable full of horses. The thrill of taking a fence that lesser horses balked at. The cool of the pond at Switherton on a hot August day. That last one wrenched his heart, because Switherton was no longer his. It would never be his again.

He tried to steer his mind in less painful directions, thinking of pleasant things about life in York. The glory of the Minster, on the rare Sundays when he went to divine service there rather than his own parish. The cheerful bustle on the streets in the early morning, when people still had a spring in their step and a hope for the day. The… His mind ran blank. The toasted cheese he made for himself in his room after work on days when he was short of funds? Ugh, no!

But he liked the strong medicinal smell of the compounding room of the apothecary shop, though it had nauseated him before he got used to it. The feel of a simple charm going right, with that strange mental *click* that well-worked magic produced. The relief of seeing a customer whose condition improved after using a treatment he had prepared.

"All done, sir," Collins said cheerfully. "Now, what would you say to getting dressed today?"

"Yes, I ought to do that."

Maybe wearing his best clothes would give him the confidence to face Miss Ainsworth and remind her that she had been talking nonsense last night. He changed his nightshirt for a clean linen shirt, let Collins pick out his handsomest waistcoat (out of date, because it was from the time Henry thought of as "before," but still attractive), and a muslin cravat. He refused to don a topcoat, though. Why bother with that when he could not leave his room?

After he breakfasted, he sat in bed working on the translation of the spellbook. He had made progress, but it was clear he could not finish this work before his leg healed. Today he made little headway. Most of his powers of thought were occupied with the task of working out what to say to Miss Ainsworth when she visited him. He would probably not see her until the afternoon, but he could not stop fretting about it.

To his surprise, she rapped at his door shortly after breakfast. This time, he recognized her knock. He had, in fact, known it was her by the sound of her footsteps outside the door. Strange how welcome that sound had become. No, what was he thinking? Not "welcome." Familiar, that was all. Her footsteps were familiar. But it was not as if he *wanted* to hear them!

"Good morning, Mr. Dawson." Miss Ainsworth entered the room, but instead of shutting the door all the way, she left it open a crack. Henry eyed it doubtfully, knowing that the draft in the hall would eventually slam the door shut.

"You should close that," he advised.

To his surprise, she blushed and shook her head. "I can't. The servants will talk."

Henry snorted. "Talk about what? Your attempts to seduce me? None of them know that." Thank goodness for that, too!

Miss Ainsworth bit her lip and clasped her hands together. She looked nervous. Henry felt a smile tug on the corners of his mouth. He knew why she felt nervous. She was about to apologize for the offer she made last night. No doubt she found it hard to admit when she was wrong. Perhaps he could help her by apologizing first, as a gentleman should.

"Miss Ainsworth," he said quietly. "I very much regret some of the things I said to you last night. Some of the language that I used was most improper. I ought not to have spoken with you in such a way. Will you forgive me?" He fell silent, waiting for her to utter her own apology. Or at least for her to accept his apology.

Instead of doing so, she gulped and twisted her hands together. "Perhaps I should shut the door after all," she whispered.

He watched, puzzled, as she softly shut the door. His

stomach sank as he began to suspect that he was about to hear something other than an apology. Something that he would not like hearing.

"Won't you please take a seat?" He tried to keep his voice polite, despite his trepidation.

"No, thank you," she said, equally politely. "I am more comfortable standing just now." That baffled Henry, who felt that it did not bode well for the conversation. "I am sorry for how I spoke to you, too. What I tried to persuade you to do. It was very wrong of me." She looked down at the floor. "I wish that we could pretend none of it ever happened."

"We can," Henry assured her. "I will not tell a soul, I promise."

She shook her head. Henry was shocked to see her eyes fill up with tears. "It is too late. I already told someone." She reached a hand up to dab at her eyes. Henry reached automatically for a pocket handkerchief, but he had not thought to ask Collins for one.

"You *what*?" Fortunately, he remembered the need to be quiet. He spoke in a harsh whisper rather than the shout he would have liked to use. "Why?"

"One of the servants saw me leave your room last night," she said, sniffling a little. "And they have already started gossiping. So, to make my aunt feel better, I told her we are engaged."

"You told her we are engaged," Henry repeated, feeling as if he had been struck on the head. "Why?"

"I told you! She was very worried. She asked me if you had declared yourself. And I told her you had."

"But I didn't!" Henry protested. "I mean, you tried to trick me into an engagement with you. But I never actually proposed."

Miss Ainsworth stopped wiping her eyes. Instead, she put her hands on her hips and glared at him. "I didn't trick you!" Her voice rose to a dangerous volume. "You asked if I wanted to marry you, and I said yes. That wasn't a trick. You need to watch your words more carefully."

Henry frowned and shook his head. "Don't try to pin this on me—this was all your doing! And now your aunt thinks we're engaged?"

"Yes. She said she would write to Uncle Elwood today."

"*Merde!*" Elwood Ainsworth was rather important in magical circles in York. He could be an ally to Henry in finding work once his leg healed, or he could be a formidable enemy if crossed. Uncle Elwood would, quite likely, be delighted with the engagement, and very much otherwise than delighted when he found out it was a fraud.

"I can speak French, you know," Miss Ainsworth reminded Henry. "I know what you just said."

"Well, since you're going to be my wife, you had better get used to my profanity now." Then he exploded, forgetting the need for silence. "Damn it, Emma, what possessed you to say that? You don't want to marry me!"

She cringed—no doubt unused to men yelling at her or swearing—and looked at the floor. "I didn't know what else to do. I had to say *something* to calm Aunt Mary down."

"What are you going to do to fix things?" Henry asked, quieting down a little. He felt ashamed of having lost his temper. Miss Ainsworth looked rather cowed now. He did not like seeing her that way. It was not like her to be shamefaced or sheepish. Usually, she exuded confidence.

"I don't know," she said. "I was hoping you would have some ideas." She smiled a hopeful, wavering smile.

Henry groaned. "Oh no! This was *your* doing! You have to figure out how to get us out of this mess."

She muttered something, so softly he could not hear her. Really, who was this timid girl who had replaced the termagant he had quarreled with last night?

"I didn't hear that," he said. "Can you come closer?"

She crept closer to the bed, taking a seat on the chair next to it. He still had to lean sideways to catch her words as she whispered, "I said, would it be so terrible to be married to me?"

Oh, God! How could he possibly answer such a question? Henry's heart smote him. "Of course, it wouldn't be *terrible*. I mean, there would be some things that would be good." Like finally getting to kiss her. Like getting to see what she looked like without so many layers of clothing. "Any man would be happy to be married to you." That wasn't exactly true, but it seemed like a thing that needed to be said. "The problem is, Emma, we would fight like cats and dogs. You know we would. Would you really be happy that way?"

"I don't know," she said, "but at least then my uncle would stop trying to introduce me to strange men."

Henry laughed bitterly. As far as silver linings went, that one was rather thin.

"I hate meeting strangers!" She spoke with a savageness that silenced his laughter. "You have no idea how terrible it is to watch their expressions change when they see me, or to sense their emotions while they try to decide if I am tolerable enough to marry for the sake of my fortune." She shook her head and looked away for a moment. "Anyway, you are right that we would fight all the time. But our marriage would make my aunt and uncle happy."

"Emma," Henry said gently, "you cannot marry just to please your relatives."

Which was errant nonsense, and he knew it. Girls married to please their relatives all the time. How many heiresses were allowed to marry their heart's desire? Precious few, unless they were lucky enough to have their heart's desire contained within the narrow circle of acceptable suitors. But whatever other girls might do, Emma deserved better.

"We will find a better solution. I promise." He had no idea how he could make good on such a promise.

"I am so very sorry for ruining things." She spoke softly and politely now. She kept looking down, so he could not see her eyes, but he thought she might be on the verge of crying again. Sure enough, he heard something like a hiccup. He felt certain it was actually a sob.

Henry had comforted crying women before. He had had to do a lot of it two years ago. He had comforted his mother after his father's death. He had comforted Mary Kingsley when she tearfully agreed to break things off. And he had comforted his sister when they left Switherton—and her beloved pony—for good.

"Come here." He extended his arm toward her.

Emma lifted her eyes and stared at him blankly. "What?" She looked at him with all the astonishment she might display to an angel who had floated down from the heavens holding a pair of stone tablets.

"Come here," he repeated.

When she still did not understand, he leaned over as

far as he could and scooped her out of her chair, as if she were a toddler who had hurt herself and needed a hug. He meant to deposit her on the bed next to him, but somehow he misjudged things, and she ended up on his lap.

He tensed up, fully expecting her to box his ears or slap him for his forwardness. Instead, very much to his surprise, she leaned against his chest, tucking her head under his chin. Cautiously, he wrapped one arm around her and with the other patted her gently on the shoulder. That was what you were supposed to do when someone was crying, wasn't it?

"That feels nice." Emma's voice sounded muffled, because she was speaking into his waistcoat. "You really do have good shields, you know. I can't tell what you're thinking at all, even though you're touching me."

Henry could say nothing in response. He sat still, petrified by shock. The girl on his lap smelled like lavender and felt as precious and fragile as a crystal chandelier, and he had absolutely no idea what he was doing. Something had just changed, and he felt too terrified to ask himself what. He did not want to know.

Instead of attempting to speak, he lowered his head so he could smell more clearly the lavender soap she used—or was it lavender water? He had no idea what kinds of scents women wore. Either way, it smelled pleasant—not exotic or dashing but comforting and homely.

At last, feeling like he had to say *something*, he whispered, "It would not be terrible to be married to you."

Emma did not answer. Perhaps she had not heard him? A suspicion suddenly struck him. To confirm it, he reached down to lift her chin up slightly so that he could see her face. Yes, she had fallen asleep on his lap, like an overtired child.

The proper thing to do would be to wake her. If she were found here, asleep in his arms—he did not want even to imagine the furor that would result. He would be lucky if he escaped being horsewhipped. And there would be no escaping matrimony if they were caught like this. Perhaps he would not have minded so much for himself, but Emma deserved better.

He really ought to wake her up and shoo her out of the room before someone came to check on him. Collins tended to drop in during the middle of the day to see if Henry needed assistance. Sometimes a maid popped in to tidy up. Occasionally Aunt Mary dropped by with a newspaper or periodical she thought might be of interest. Really, anyone could come in.

Henry looked down at Emma and sighed. He could no more wake her than he could have woken a sleeping baby. Instead, he sat perfectly still, holding her in his arms and frantically trying to think of a solution for this mess. But no solution came to mind, and Emma's warm weight leaning against him made it difficult to concentrate on anything else. Eventually, he fell asleep, too.

Chapter Twelve

Emma awoke, wondering why she felt so stiff. How had she fallen asleep half-sitting like this? She yawned, and sat up, and as she did so, the top of her head banged into something hard.

"Ouch! That was my chin!" She looked up, startled, and what she saw confused her even more. Mr. Dawson glared down at her, rubbing his chin.

"What are you doing here?" In her confusion, she had no idea why she was sitting on his lap, with one of his arms tucked around her.

"This is my room! I'm taking a nap here! Where else would I be? It's not as if I could leave." He spoke in a harsh whisper, presumably not wanting anyone to overhear them talking.

Emma looked around, puzzled. Yes, this was the guest room assigned to Mr. Dawson. A tasteful blue-and-green floral wallpaper covered the walls. There were no curtains on the four-poster bed. Aunt Mary disapproved of bedcurtains, believing they stopped the flow of fresh air. Emma had had to fight tooth and nail to get the decorative curtains on her own bed, and if Uncle Elwood had not suggested that they compromise and order curtains of lace, she might not have gotten them at all.

Now that she thought about it, she remembered coming here to break the news of the supposed engagement to Mr. Dawson. And she remembered him trying to comfort her. But she still did not entirely understand how his attempt to soothe her had ended with them asleep together.

"If I get caught here, we'll really be in trouble," she noted.

"But they think we're already engaged," Mr. Dawson pointed out. "What more can they do to us?"

"Make us get married right away," Emma suggested. It took about a month to marry using banns, but if one got a license from the bishop, there was no wait. It would be very like Aunt Mary to insist that she marry Mr. Dawson immediately. Then Emma brightened, as she realized that would not be possible. "Of course, you couldn't go to church to get married until your leg heals. That buys us some time." Hopefully, she would be able to think of a reason for breaking the engagement without upsetting Aunt Mary too much.

"Unless your uncle applies for a special license, so we could get married here in this room," he pointed out. Unlike a common license, a special license allowed people to marry in any location, at any time of day, not just in a church.

"Goodness, you're right. He could do that." Special licenses were not usually granted to commoners, but one could plead special circumstances, such as a broken leg that prevented a man from going to church to marry.

Emma did not think Uncle Elwood would want to go all the way to London to apply for a license at Doctor's Commons. But what if Aunt Mary begged him to do it? He sometimes gave in to her whims. Though the two were not related, they had known each other so long they sometimes acted like siblings.

"It does sound like the sort of thing Aunt Mary

would suggest." She shivered at the idea. "We'd better hope she doesn't find us like this."

"In that case, *why are you still sitting on my lap*?" he hissed right in her ear.

"Oh!" For some reason, it had not even occurred to Emma to question her own behavior. She scrambled off the bed so quickly she tumbled onto the floor.

"Are you trying to break one of *your* bones?" He spoke sarcastically, but he acted helpfully, twisting his upper body so he could lean down and offer her a hand up.

Emma scrambled to her feet and tried to straighten out her dress. It had been wrinkled from her sleep in it, and now it was dirtied from the floor. Evidently the maids were not doing a good job of keeping Mr. Dawson's room clean.

"I am fine," Emma said. "Just a mess."

"People will take one look at you and assume you have been tumbling with me on the floor," he said sourly. "You had better fix your hair before anyone sees you."

A flush rose on Emma's face. She glared at Mr. Dawson, hating him for embarrassing her, and hating even more the fact that he was right. She did need to fix her hair before she ran into anyone. The servants would all be suspicious and ready to pounce on any sign that she had been misbehaving, thanks to the gossip about her late-night visit.

She stalked over to the dressing table. The mirror here was not as big as the one in her room, but she could still see well enough to take her hair out of the messy bun and re-do it as best she could. Somehow, she had lost a few hairpins.

"So," Mr. Dawson said as she worked on her hair.

"What are we going to do to get out of this engagement you've trapped us in?"

Emma sighed. She had hoped he would not ask about that just yet. "I will think of something." She opened her mouth to explain that she was good at solving problems, then thought better of it. That would just give Mr. Dawson a chance to argue with her. "We will get out of this, I promise. In the meantime, I had better get away from you before someone finds us." He nodded his agreement.

She opened the door a crack so she could peer up and down the corridor. No one was in sight, so she slipped out of the room and down toward her own room. She shut herself in her room, turned the lock, and collapsed into the armchair by the empty fireplace.

She had done her best to project confidence when talking to her supposed fiancé, but now that she was alone, she wilted. She had absolutely no idea how to get out of this mess. As the bride, she would have to be the one to end the engagement. A groom could not break things off. But she could not imagine what she could tell Aunt Mary to explain breaking off the engagement.

Could she uncover some dark secret from Mr. Dawson's past that made him ineligible as a husband? Or, rather, could she invent a fictitious dark secret? Emma felt confident in her own powers of invention. The problem was that whatever she came up with would have to be something that could not be disproven—and hadn't Uncle Elwood already looked into her suitor's background? She had the impression, from a few offhanded remarks Uncle Elwood had made, that he had thoroughly investigated Mr. Dawson before introducing him to Emma.

Moreover, if Emma spread a false rumor about Mr. Dawson's character, it might ruin his chances of advancing in his career. All it would take would be Uncle Elwood talking to the wrong people in York, and Mr. Dawson would find himself blackballed from the magical community.

Maybe it would be better to find an objection on Emma's side, then. Rather than proving that Mr. Dawson was in some way unsuitable, could she come up with a good reason why she did not want to marry at all? Emma sighed. The problem here was that her aunt and uncle had already heard her reasons against an arranged marriage and dismissed them. Perhaps she could simply say she had been mistaken about her own heart. That happened sometimes, didn't it? She would just have to figure out how to convince her aunt and uncle that she meant it when she said she had made a mistake in accepting Mr. Dawson's proposal.

Emma went to bed that night thinking she had plenty of time to fix this problem. But in the coming days, events were set in motion far more quickly than she had imagined possible. A mere two days after the supposed engagement, their seamstress arrived from Whitby with a book of fabric samples, a notebook, and her tape measure. She took Emma's measurements, not that they had changed since the last time she was fitted for clothing, and then she conferred with Aunt Mary about the bride clothes. Miss Richardson suggested silver for the wedding dress, and Aunt Mary happily concurred.

"Isn't that rather too flashy for me?" Emma tried to suggest.

She could not picture herself in a dress of silver lamé over tissue. But she was overruled—or rather, simply ignored. She bit her lip and reminded herself that since she was not really going to marry Mr. Dawson, it did not matter what the wedding dress looked like. But she felt increasingly ashamed of the amount of money that would go into these clothes she would never have reason to use.

Time to begin sowing hints of doubt to prepare her aunt for the moment when she broke the engagement.

"I hope I am doing the right thing in marrying Mr. Dawson," she said to Aunt Mary after the seamstress had left. She forced herself to wrinkle her brow as if deeply concerned. In fact, very little dissembling was required on her part. She *was* deeply concerned about how to get out of this absurd situation.

"Oh, my dear, you have nothing to fret about." Aunt Mary patted her hand kindly. "Your uncle did an excellent job of investigating Mr. Dawson before he introduced him, so you need have no doubt about the young man's character. And I am sure it is clear he is a very pleasant gentleman. Few other men would be as patient about being confined to the sickroom as he is."

Emma tried shifting tactics slightly, to see if a different angle might be more successful. "Perhaps it is not Mr. Dawson I am worried about, but the state of matrimony."

To her surprise, Aunt Mary nodded. "That is perfectly natural. Marrying is a great change for a woman. I will have Mrs. Elcott come and talk to you about it."

"Mrs. Elcott?" Emma repeated, confused. She did not see what the vicar's wife had to do with the question at all. It was not as if she had theological concerns about the marriage service in the prayer book.

Before she could figure that out, she had to face a

much larger problem—Uncle Elwood. Naturally, he came up from York on Friday evening, armed with a list of things that had to be done to settle Emma's fortune properly. And, to Emma's horror, he was absolutely thrilled about the engagement. She could not remember ever seeing him so full of smiles.

She was the first to greet him in the drawing room, and since they were alone, she prepared herself to start dropping hints about backing out of the engagement. She even toyed with the idea of telling him the truth, on the grounds that he was less likely to be scandalized by it than Aunt Mary.

But before she could say anything, Uncle Elwood embraced her, patting her on the back. "I am so happy that you and Henry were able to work things out!"

Her uncle had good mental shields, but while she touched him, Emma could pick up the satisfaction and relief rolling off him. Why relief? She cocked her head and narrowed her eyes, wondering what he had to be relieved about. But once Uncle Elwood stepped away from her, all she could read was the smile on his face.

"He is a fine young man, and familiar with life in the country," her uncle continued. "He will do well managing Westwinds for you."

Emma frowned. Was that why Uncle Elwood felt so relieved? Because he would no longer have to help manage her estate while also running his own wizarding practice?

"I can manage Westwinds." She knew all the tenants by name and reputation, if not by face. And Purdy served as steward of the estate, as well as manager of the home farm. She knew she could work well with him, if given the chance.

"You will have other things to think of by and by." Her uncle must have seen how confused Emma felt, because he clarified, "I know you like children, and I am sure you will soon have your hands full with your own family."

Emma's mouth dropped open. This was getting out of hand. "Uncle Elwood," she began, "I need to tell you something."

But before she could blurt out the truth, Aunt Mary bustled into the room, asking questions about Uncle Elwood's journey and catching him up to date on the progress that had already been made ordering Emma's trousseau. Before Emma knew what was going on, she had been shooed out of the room so that Aunt Mary and Uncle Elwood could confer alone for a moment.

"Go and tell Mr. Dawson that your uncle is here," Aunt Mary recommended. "Uncle Elwood will naturally want to talk to your intended."

Emma trudged up the staircase, feeling more worried with every step she took. She slowed down, dragging out the walk, because she knew Mr. Dawson would want to know her plan, and she did not have a plan. She had known it might be difficult to break an engagement. She had not realized, though, that her guardians would simply brush aside her objections, as if her opinion of the engagement did not matter. Did she really not matter after all? Was it only her fortune that counted for anything?

She tapped on Mr. Dawson's door but did not bother waiting for a response before she opened it. Thus, she caught him in the act of folding a newspaper into a paper hat.

"What in the world are you doing?" she asked,

directing all her frustration with her relatives at him. He made an easy target, being as big as a barn and just as stationary.

"Haven't you ever heard of knocking?" He put the paper hat on his head, crossed his arms, and scowled at her. The jaunty angle of the folded paper might have suggested he was in a playful mood, but the glower on his face contradicted that assumption.

Emma was so used to him glaring at her that she simply ignored his scowl, returning to her earlier question. "Why do you have that ridiculous thing on your head?"

His face relaxed a little, and a faint grin replaced his scowl. "I am preparing for a career as a pirate. That is how I will restore my family fortune."

Emma rolled her eyes. "Well, I wish you success in that venture." If there were pirates operating off the coast of Yorkshire, that would be a surprise to her, but anything was possible. "If you're that bored, why don't you work on the translation?"

"I did, until my hand cramped." He shrugged. "I don't see how clerks can stand to write all day."

"They probably get arthritis young." Then Emma shook her head. They had more important things to talk about. "My uncle is here. He wants to talk to you."

"What have you told him about the engagement?" Mr. Dawson asked.

"He didn't give me a chance to say anything." Emma sank down onto the chair next to the bed, sighing. "No one seems to care what I say. I don't know how I'm going to fix this mess."

"Run away," he advised her.

"What? How would that solve anything? And where

would I go?"

He shrugged. "I don't know. Run off to the Orkneys or something. Some little island in the middle of nowhere. They can't make you get married if you're not here."

"It would be too easy to track me," Emma said sourly. "A young lady with pockmarks on her face, traveling alone? People would remember me wherever I went." More to the point, there was no way she could stand traveling on a public stagecoach. The emotions of the other passengers would overwhelm her. She would likely either faint or get sick to her stomach, or both.

"I would offer to run away with you, but I can't really leave the room at the moment. And," he added, turning his paper hat to a new angle, "I am not sure that doing so would really help the situation."

"It would make it a hundred times worse," Emma agreed. "We'd have to get married, and there would be a scandal. And my family would worry. What are you doing to that hat?"

"I'm trying to turn it into a paper boat. I used to know how to fold paper into a boat." The newspaper did not cooperate with him on this, perhaps because it had already been folded into a hat. Its integrity as a piece of paper had been challenged.

"I wish you would focus," Emma grumbled. "I am running out of ideas. I could use your help figuring out how to break this engagement."

"I don't believe you ever had an idea," he said heartlessly. "You thought you could just back out, didn't you? But your uncle has been trying to get you married for years. He isn't going to let you weasel out of it now." He returned the newspaper to its hat form and put it back on his head. It looked rather worse for wear.

A week ago, Emma would have vigorously defended Uncle Elwood. She had always believed that her guardian had her best interests at heart, even when she did not see eye to eye with him. Now, she suspected that Mr. Dawson was right. Uncle Elwood and Aunt Mary would not want her to end a desirable engagement on a whim.

"Maybe I should just tell the truth?" she suggested. She nibbled on her thumbnail as she thought.

"Which part of the truth, though? The part where you tried to get me to be your fancy man? The part where you tried to entrap me into a fake engagement? The part where you really *did* entrap me in a fake engagement? The part where you slept in my bed for hours?" Mr. Dawson looked prepared to keep listing her humiliating actions for days.

"Oh, do be quiet," Emma snapped. *Must* he remind her of all the ridiculous things she had done? Though the falling asleep in his bed was entirely his fault, anyway. He had been the one who pulled her onto his lap. She would never have done such a thing on her own.

She bit all the way through her poor abused thumbnail, and stared down at her hand, surprised. She thought she had given up that habit years ago. It must be a sign of how stressed she felt, that she had taken it up again.

"Obviously I will not tell my uncle the whole truth. But I will tell him the engagement is a lie. I had better tell him now. Maybe there will still be time to cancel the order for my bride clothes." Her stomach churned uneasily at the thought of that conversation. Uncle Elwood would be so disappointed in her.

"Keep the bride clothes," Mr. Dawson advised. "You'll need them for the next time your uncle tries to make a match for you. He's going to keep doing it until you finally cave in and marry someone, you know." He was probably right about that.

Mr. Dawson opened his mouth to say something else, but they both jumped when they heard a knock on the door. Emma recognized that knock. She bit her lip and tried to send a speaking glance Mr. Dawson's way, but he just looked puzzled.

"Come in," he called, and Uncle Elwood entered the room.

Uncle Elwood had a pleasant smile on his face, but it faltered as soon as his eyes met Emma's. He shook his head. "Emma, you need to leave the door open when you visit your fiancé. People will draw assumptions that you would not like." Emma's face began to burn with shame.

"It was my fault, Uncle Elwood," Mr. Dawson said. "I wanted to read Emma some of my poetry, and I didn't want anyone to overhear." Somehow, he managed to cultivate a bashful look as he confessed, "I don't like sharing my poems with other people, but I make an exception for Emma."

He gave her the most unbelievably syrupy look, which contrasted strangely with the paper hat he still wore on his head. Emma had to turn a giggle into a cough, so as not to give away the lie. Mr. Dawson deserved high marks for creativity. She would not have thought of that story. At least not on such short notice.

"Be that as it may, Emma ought not to be in here with the door shut," Uncle Elwood said. "You may be engaged, but you are not married yet." He sighed. "Really, Emma ought to have a chaperone when she is in here, but I suppose, under the circumstances, the rules can be bent a little." Then he smiled benevolently. "I think we can plan on a wedding as soon as Henry is well enough to come to the church, so you need not wait that long."

Emma drew in a deep breath. She needed to tell the truth, and she needed to do it now, before Uncle Elwood made any further plans. "Uncle Elwood, I wonder if I could speak to you for a moment?"

It would be easier to confess the truth about the engagement if she could talk to her uncle alone, without anyone else to witness her embarrassment. Eventually, of course, Aunt Mary would have to know, too, but she hoped her uncle could help break the news.

"Of course, Emma," he said cheerfully. "I will talk to you after dinner. But just now I need to speak to Mr. Dawson about some business matters. If you could excuse us?" And just like that, Emma once again found herself ushered out of the room by her uncle, who closed the door firmly behind her.

Chapter Thirteen

Emma was never going to confess the truth to her uncle, that much seemed clear. And it was equally clear that she was not entirely at fault for that. Her uncle seemed determined not to listen to her objections. But perhaps he would listen to Henry.

"Mr. Ainsworth," Henry said, retreating to a formality he had long since left behind, "there is something you should know."

"I don't want to know," Emma's uncle said at once. "Whatever you and Emma have really been doing in here—and I don't for one minute believe you were reading poetry together—I do not want to know the details."

He gave Henry a quizzical look, at which point Henry realized he still had a paper hat on his head. Henry's hand twitched, eager to yank it off and crumple it up, but that would make it look like he was ashamed to be caught wearing it. Better to brave it out, although the hat did make it difficult to keep a serious expression on his face as he listened to Emma's uncle.

"Whatever you have done does not matter, since you are marrying her. But…" Uncle Elwood narrowed his eyes. "You had better marry her, young man. Do you understand?"

"We have not done anything like what you are implying," Henry snapped. "You really don't know your

134

niece if you think her capable of such behavior." True, Emma had tried to seduce him. But there was certainly no reason why her uncle should ever know that.

"I know human nature." Uncle Elwood sat down on the wooden chair beside Henry's bed and leaned back a little, as if settling in for a long discussion. "And I know that a broken limb need not stop a determined man from—"

"Anyway," Henry interrupted, not wanting to hear the details of what Uncle Elwood thought a man could or couldn't do with a broken leg, "the fact of the matter is that we are not really engaged. Emma lied about that to calm her aunt down." It had been a ridiculous lie, and he still could not understand why she had said such a thing. Did she *want* to ruin both their lives?

"I don't think you understand," Uncle Elwood said calmly. "Whatever you and Emma did or did not agree to, the two of you need to get married. Servants talk, and gossip spreads quickly. If you don't marry, everyone in the parish will talk about how Emma lost her virtue to a house guest, and they will bring the story up whenever her name comes into conversation, for the rest of her life. You have ruined her, young man, and you owe it to her to marry her."

"I did not ruin her!" Henry had, in fact, gone to some trouble to avoid it. True, that had partly been because he found her offer insulting, but that had not been his only objection. "And that is a stupid reason for two people to get married. Emma deserves better than that. I won't do it. And yes," he added, before Uncle Elwood could threaten him, "I know that you can make my life miserable in York. You can ruin my career if you want. But the fact of the matter is that Emma does not want to marry me, and I am not going to marry an unwilling bride."

He expected Uncle Elwood to respond harshly. But Emma's uncle surprised him with a smug smile. "You are a young man of character, and I admire that about you, Henry. But you are wrong about Emma. Whatever reticence she might feel about it now, she will be very happy with you. Since your only objection is about Emma's willingness to marry you, let me assure you that I will talk to her about it in due time. Let *me* worry about that."

Henry shook his head at this. He felt certain Uncle Elwood was the one who misunderstood Emma. If he really thought he could persuade Emma into doing something she was determined not to do, he must be deluded.

Uncle Elwood did not give Henry a chance to respond, instead taking the conversation in a different direction. "You need to worry about taking charge of the estate. Emma inherited a significant amount of money from her mother, invested in the Funds, so although the land attached to Westwinds is not extensive, you will be looking at an income of about four thousand a year, give or take a little. Naturally, the fortune and the land will be held in trust for Emma, but you will have to manage the income, and—"

"Why don't you let Emma manage it herself?" Henry could not believe his ears. He had just told Uncle Elwood that he refused to marry Emma, and yet the man continued to prate about income!

"If you wish to give her control of the income, you may," Uncle Elwood replied, shrugging his shoulders. "And of course, we will make provisions in the marriage contract for adequate pin money. But I suspect the tenants will want to deal directly with you. It is a pity that I cannot take you on a tour of the estate to meet the tenants, but that will have to wait until you heal. Let me talk to you about the home farm first. You will, of course, have met Purdy?"

Henry nodded, having no idea what he could say to put an end to this farce. To his horror, Uncle Elwood spent the better part of an hour discussing the farm attached to Westwinds and the improvements that might be made in the near future. If Henry were really going to marry Emma and manage the estate for her, he would no doubt have gained considerable useful information from this lecture.

But, under the circumstances, all he could think about was how they were going to get out of this situation. Maybe Emma really would have to run away from home. Henry found that he had grossly underestimated the force of Uncle Elwood's character. Or, to put it more bluntly, his pigheadedness. It must be an Ainsworth family trait. Certainly, Emma had inherited it as well.

Henry's only comfort was the knowledge that they could not get married at all until his broken leg healed. He anticipated being stuck in bed for more than a month yet. But on Monday, after Uncle Elwood had gone back to York, Dr. Thomas came to see him.

"I've got something new to try," the physician announced. He walked with a spring to his step this morning. "A very powerful potion that can accelerate bone healing. Only German apothecaries know how to make it, but I was lucky enough to get one of my old colleagues to send me some from Berlin. We might have you out of bed and moving about on crutches in a week or two."

"What?" Henry stared, stricken with horror. A week ago, this would have been the best news he had ever heard, as it would have signaled the end of his imprisonment. Now it heralded the ringing of wedding bells. If he and Emma were madly in love, this would be cause for celebration. Instead, he felt sick to his stomach. He could not stand to see Emma trapped in an unwanted marriage, but he did not know how to get out of it.

"I'm sure your fiancée will be glad to hear that, too," Dr. Thomas said.

The knowing smile on his face made Henry want to kick him down the stairs. Naturally, everyone would assume that Henry and Emma would be eager to marry.

The physician pulled a large glass bottle out of his bag. "Keep this out of direct sunlight," he advised, "and do not take more than one teaspoonful a day. It tastes terrible, I know, but the best medicine often does."

"Thank you." Henry tried to sound as if he felt genuinely grateful. He was undoubtedly very fortunate to receive cutting-edge medical care. He knew that. But did this mean that he and Emma had only a week or two to come up with an escape plan? Running away was beginning to look like their only option.

Then again, it took time to post banns. Emma's bride clothes would take time to make, too. The wedding dress was not yet finished. Perhaps there was no rush. He clung to that hope. He spent a good deal of time that day thinking about the problem, because he had no way to take his mind off it. Uncle Elwood had taken away the spellbook Henry had been translating and replaced it with a stack of account books going back decades.

"Your time would be better spent learning about the estate," he told Henry cheerfully.

Again, if Henry and Emma really intended to marry, those account books might have been useful in giving Henry a better understanding of his new responsibilities. But, given the actual situation, Henry could imagine nothing more boring or more useless than flipping through them.

Worst of all, Collins had moved Henry's stack of novels to make room for the account books. The novels now perched on the edge of the dressing table, out of Henry's reach. If he wanted to read one, he would have to ring for a servant to bring it to him.

Uncle Elwood left more than account books behind for Henry. Before he drove off in his gig, he dropped a purse full of guineas on Henry's bedside table.

"You may wish to purchase new dress clothes for the wedding," he explained.

Heat rose on Henry's cheeks at the implicit criticism of his clothing—all of which was at least two years old. If he were to get married, he *would* need new clothes. The master of Westwinds would be expected to dress the part. And if Emma were to stand before the altar in a ridiculously expensive silver lamé dress, he could hardly shame her by wearing out-of-date and worn-out morning clothes. He sighed but did not utter any protests.

After Uncle Elwood left, Henry stared at that bag of gold, feeling such a mixture of greed and guilt that it nearly nauseated him. He could not, in good conscience, spend any of that money. And yet, the things he could do with it! He could save some of it for the next time his mother overspent her own income. He could buy himself a better pair of shoes when the soles of his current pair gave out. He could *eat at a pub* instead of toasting bread and cheese alone in his room.

Or he could be an honorable man and leave the money behind when he left Westwinds, on the grounds that he had done nothing to earn it. Henry needed no one to tell him that would be the right thing to do. But it broke his heart to picture himself walking away from a pile of gold when he had so many uses for it.

He tried to distract himself from it by flipping through an account book, but that proved every bit as uninteresting as he had imagined—and whoever kept the book had had terrible handwriting, to boot. If Henry were master here, he would at least make sure the records were legible to future generations! A dangerous line of thought. Emma did not want to marry him. He would never be the master of Westwinds. He ought always to keep that in mind.

With Uncle Elwood gone, there was no one to share a glass of port with Henry after dinner. He used that time to think, instead, and by the time Emma rapped at his door—long after the rest of the house had gone to bed—he knew what he had to do. He did not like it, but he saw no way around it. Consequently, he was scowling when Emma walked into the room, shutting the door behind her.

"Didn't your uncle tell you to leave the door open?" Henry raised his eyebrows at his supposed fiancée.

"They're already forcing us to get married. What more can they do?" She shuddered as she sat down on the chair. "I already had to listen to the vicar's wife explain how babies are made."

"Didn't you already know that?"

"Yes, but I told Aunt Mary that I had reservations

about the state of matrimony, and she assumed that was what I meant." She pulled a rather childish face in disgust. "It wasn't as if Mrs. Elcott could answer my one real question, anyway."

"What? She couldn't explain what a French letter is?"

To his delight, Emma turned scarlet and scowled at him. "How did you know I asked that? Are *you* a mind reader now?" Henry chuckled, pleased at having gotten even more of a reaction than he had hoped for. "She told me what that was," Emma admitted, "although she seemed horrified that I had even heard of it. I guess it's not the sort of thing a well-bred young lady is supposed to have heard of."

Henry laughed even harder, amused at the thought that he had corrupted Emma. She shook her head at him. But he thought he saw the corner of her mouth curl up, as if she too were amused. If only talking to Emma could always be this fun! They had, he remembered, had some very pleasant conversations while they played chess or backgammon together—before she ruined things by trying to seduce him.

"Anyway," she continued, "what I really wanted to ask her about is how an empath could tolerate being that physically close to another person for a prolonged period of time."

"It wouldn't necessarily be a prolonged period of time. That would depend on the man." Henry knew at least that much. Young men gossiped rather more freely about bedroom matters than women appeared to do.

"I don't even want to know what you mean." Emma glared at him again. "But anyway, there would be no way Mrs. Elcott would know the answer to that question, so I didn't ask."

"Could you ask another empath?" Henry suspected the answer was no. Emma was too smart not to have thought of that already. He was not surprised when she shook her head.

"I don't know any empaths as sensitive as I am. And some empaths have their own shields, so they can protect themselves from other people's emotions. I can't do that." She sighed and looked down at her hands. "I have a particularly unfortunate combination of sensitivity and weak defenses. That is what makes life so hard for me."

Henry had wondered about that. Empathy, being a form of magecraft, was a rarer magical gift than wizardry or sorcery, but he had never heard of an empath who had to live in seclusion the way Emma did. At one point, he had speculated that she might use her empathy as an excuse to hide her scarred face. But he had come to see that her problem was real, not an excuse of any kind. Those simple Ladies' Aid Society visits visibly exhausted her.

"I am sorry." And then, because he did genuinely sympathize with her, he admitted something he might have otherwise kept to himself. "I see why you planned to experiment before you got married." His religious principles told him that people were supposed to remain chaste outside of marriage, but he did not know how else she was likely to find an answer to her question.

Emma's head snapped up, and she stared at him as if surprised. Then she nibbled on her thumbnail. That gesture made Henry a little nervous. Surely, she couldn't be thinking…?

"You know," Emma said slowly, "my uncle and aunt seem determined to force us to marry."

"Yes, they do," Henry said cautiously. "Determined" seemed too weak a word to him. But he did not like the speculative gleam in Emma's eyes. He knew she was scheming something he wouldn't like. "Your uncle is rather stubborn." As much as he wanted to tell Emma that she had obviously inherited the same trait, he restrained himself. He was very much afraid he would need all his strength for whatever Emma said next. "But I think I know how to get out of this engagement."

"You can tell me that later." She waved her hand dismissively, though her eyes did not leave his face for a second. "Just now, breaking the engagement is beside the point."

Henry raised his eyebrows. "I rather thought that was the whole problem?"

"It may be the whole problem for you," she granted, "but not for me. As you pointed out, even if we break off our engagement, my uncle is probably going to keep matchmaking for me."

"Very likely." Henry's plan would get him out of the engagement, but it would not stop Uncle Elwood from looking for another suitor for his niece. He had no idea how Emma could avoid that. Maybe she couldn't.

"So it would be wise for me to figure out now whether it would even be possible to be married to someone." She clasped her hands together as if nervous, but met his eyes boldly enough.

Oh, God, not this again! Henry did not need to hear more to know where this was going. He shook his head. "I already told you no. I'm not your petticoat pensioner!"

"But we're engaged now," she pointed out. "Doesn't that make a difference?"

"If we actually intended to get married, perhaps.

Perhaps." Henry scowled. Even if they intended to marry, anticipating their vows would be scandalous. If the servants caught wind of it, the results could be disastrous…except, he realized, the servants already thought that Henry and Emma were misbehaving. "But we don't intend to marry each other."

He expected her to argue further. Instead, she just looked at him with wide eyes. He waited for her to break the silence, but she continued to stare at him. Finally, he caved and asked, "What?"

"This could be my only chance," she explained. "Where else am I going to find a single man with such good mental shields?"

Henry buried his face in his hands. He had thought this battle was over. He had thought he'd won. He was not prepared to fight the same ground all over again. His defenses were no longer strong enough. He had been thinking of having Emma in his bed for days now, and none of his reasons for resisting her indecent proposal seemed nearly as convincing as before. If he acted according to his desires, he would happily give in.

But more than his own desires were at stake here. "What if someone finds out?"

"They already think we've been in bed together," she pointed out. He sighed. He had hoped she was unaware of that. "Uncle Elwood took me aside and told me I needed to be more discreet about visiting you."

"He didn't tell you to *stop*?" Henry did not bother trying to hide how shocked he felt. What the hell kind of guardian was Uncle Elwood?

"He seemed to think that since we were getting married in a couple of weeks, it didn't matter all that much." She shrugged as if she thought this made sense.

It did not make sense to Henry. Most parents and guardians treated a young lady's chastity as if it were a priceless piece of delicate white fabric that would be ruined by the faintest smudge. There was a reason why Henry had done no more than kiss Mary Kingsley once, after all. They had rarely had a moment alone with each other.

"Under the circumstances, I don't see how it would make things worse for us to do what people already think we're doing," Emma concluded.

Henry felt certain a good rebuttal to this claim was possible, but he could not think of one. He could only think of having Emma in his arms. And touching other parts of his body. He grasped for straws, as if he could build a wall out of them that could keep their bodies apart.

"How would you make certain that you didn't fall pregnant?"

To his horror, she replied, "Would it be so bad if I did? I like babies, and—"

"Yes, it *would* be so bad!" he snapped. "I do not want to leave illegitimate children behind." That would be the height of irresponsibility, and much worse than corrupting an innocent maiden. Was Emma really innocent in any meaningful sense of the word, given her disreputable scheming?

"Very well. If I get a contraceptive charm, you'll do it?" She pierced him with a sharp, eager gaze.

Henry's jaw dropped open. "I never said that!"

Though, he realized, it seemed like a logical implication of what he had said. Damn, he needed to choose his words more carefully. He should have learned that by now. He had been at Westwinds a good two months and had spent much of the last week or two arguing with Emma. One would think he knew better than to leave any weakness open for attack.

"But will you?" She hesitated for a minute, then added, "You could always close your eyes and think about someone else, you know." She glanced away from him, staring at the pile of ledgers next to the bed as if she found decades' worth of accounts fascinating.

"Why on earth would I think of someone else?" Henry demanded. He had doubts about his ability to think at all in such circumstances, but he did not feel the need to share those doubts.

"I meant, if you didn't want to go to bed with me. I know that I do not look like most girls." She spoke matter-of-factly, as if this were just a commonly accepted truth and not a blighting self-assessment.

He could only stare. Was that what she thought? "Are you daft?" he said at last, knowing that he had to say something, but not knowing what. "You're beautiful."

She shook her head immediately. "I have a mirror, Mr. Dawson. I know perfectly well what I look like, and it isn't beautiful."

Henry chose to attack the weakest point of what she had just said. "I really think you should call me 'Henry.' Since you want to go to bed with me, I mean. You can't keep calling me 'Mr. Dawson' while you're passionately—"

"Henry, then." Her face had turned an interesting shade of red.

Henry could not help smirking a little. Emma might talk boldly, but she could be shy, too. Perhaps she was less a violent barn cat and more like a hedgehog, whose soft underbelly was rarely shown. That was the wrong metaphor to think of, though, since it just made Henry wonder what her belly looked like, and, for that matter, what the rest of her looked like under her shift. He had seen his share of pornography in school—the older boys passed it around after curfew—but a print in a book was quite different from a real, live woman.

"What are you thinking about?" she demanded, and now it was Henry's turn to blush.

"I was thinking about how beautiful you are," he said glibly. It was not entirely a lie, after all. "I mean, yes, you have scars on your face, but that doesn't change the beautiful things about you." She kept staring at him. As the silence stretched out, he realized that she did not believe him.

"Come here," he suggested, reaching his arm out for her as he had the other day. This time he did not have to lift her onto his lap. She came and settled there herself. She gave him a wary look, though, as if she did not trust his motives. She was probably right to be cautious. Henry was not sure what he was about to do either.

He tentatively reached up to stroke the side of her face. "You have such lovely eyes. I love how dark they are, and how that darkness stands out against your face." She rode and walked about the estate often enough, but perhaps because she often wore a veil over her bonnet her complexion stayed pale.

"I love your hair, too." He cautiously reached up and tugged lightly on one of her perfect ringlets. "How do you get it to curl like that when it is naturally straight?"

"Curl papers," she said with a laugh. "There is no magic to it." A faint pink blush lit up her face now, and he thought she might be starting to believe him.

"But perhaps most of all, I love your mouth." That was a lie if ever he told one. He loved her bust even more than her mouth. But he was trying not to look at her décolletage just now. If she blushed just hearing him talking about her eyes and her hair, he did not think she was at all ready to hear how much he admired her figure.

"My mouth?" she repeated, sounding startled.

"Yes," he told her. "Because I want to do this to it."

She frowned, drawing her eyebrows down. He did not let that stop him from tipping her chin up with one hand and kissing her on the lips. Her mouth was just as soft and yielding as he had imagined it would be. He brushed his lips against her mouth once, twice, three times, then paused, thinking perhaps he had trespassed enough. He was half-afraid she was going to box his ears for taking liberties.

She stared at him, wide-eyed, and gulped. "You really think I'm beautiful?" she whispered.

Henry sighed. How could she doubt him after that? He leaned forward so he could touch his forehead to hers. "If you don't believe me, see for yourself." And he dropped his mental shields so she could interpret his emotions without need for words.

Chapter Fourteen

To Emma, it felt as if she had been dropped into a rushing river of feeling, strong enough to carry her away. She gasped and pulled away from Henry, startled by the unexpected warmth of his emotions. If she had been asked a few hours ago, she would have said Henry Dawson did not like her, but by now had learned to respect her intellect. At least, so she had hoped.

But the feelings that swamped her now had little to do with her intellect, nor would they typically be considered respectful. As an empath, Emma could pick up on sensations like pain, discomfort, and hunger, but she could feel sensations of comfort and pleasure, too. She knew immediately that her supposed fiancé was literally aching with desire for her.

Her face turned scarlet as she realized that, because she still sat on his lap, only a few layers of cloth separated her from his erect…male organ of generation, as Mrs. Elcott had primly referred to it. She suspected that Henry would call it something far less proper. She scrambled off his lap, horrified beyond the scope of the word "embarrassment."

"Sorry. I suppose that was too much." Henry lowered his eyes, as if he felt embarrassed too. To her relief, he closed down his shields so she could no longer sense that tide of desire.

She remained standing, momentarily stunned into

silence. And her own body ached in interesting places, apparently as a secondhand reaction to Henry's desire.

"Do you feel like that all the time?" she squeaked, appalled at the thought.

"Of course not! Only when you're sitting on my lap, kissing me. Or," he added, sounding a little bashful, "when you're wearing that one red dress, the one with the low neckline."

Emma shook her head. Having felt his desire for herself, she could no longer doubt him. But she also could not wrap her mind around his reaction. Ever since she'd first looked in the mirror after recovering from smallpox, she had wondered if any man would ever love her. At her most optimistic, she thought there might be a man who would look past the pockmarks on her face and love her for her mind and heart. She had not expected to be desired so…fiercely…for the sake of her body alone.

And she had certainly not expected the man who wanted her so passionately to be someone as prickly and sarcastic as Henry Dawson. He had given no indication at all of such feelings. On the contrary, she had been certain he disliked her. True, there had been times during his convalescence when he behaved very pleasantly, but lately they seemed always to quarrel.

But, she reminded herself, desire and affection were two different things. Henry did not love her. He merely wanted her. If he had loved her, he would not be trying so hard to get out of their fake engagement. Still, perhaps she could use this attraction to her advantage, now that she knew about it.

Henry narrowed his eyes, looking suspicious. "Emma, what are you scheming?"

"I am not scheming anything! I just wanted to ask

you about your plan for getting out of the engagement." She hoped that would be enough to redirect his attention.

"Oh, that." His face relaxed, and he shrugged his shoulders. "I am going to run away."

Disappointment sank into her bones. "That's it? Your plan is to run away?" She had expected something more complicated. More plausible. Less childish.

He nodded. "They can't force me to marry you if I'm not here." Emma opened her mouth to start reminding him of all the things that her uncle could do to make his life unpleasant. "And," he said quickly, not giving her a chance to speak, "I will have to leave York, because your uncle will certainly make life difficult for me there. I will go to…" He paused, as if uncertain, and said, "Leeds, perhaps. Or Doncaster. Or even London!" Emma frowned. She could not have said why, but she rather thought he was lying.

"Uncle Elwood knows magicians all over England," she warned him. "He even corresponds with a wizard in Hampshire who specializes in defensive magic."

"I won't go to Hampshire, then," he said cheerfully. "And before you ask, no, I am not going to tell you where I am going. Better that you not know. That way you can't reveal it to anyone."

"As if I would!" she protested. One would think he could trust her by now.

"But this way you won't be tempted." He looked down at his leg in the cast. "I suppose I will go as soon as I can walk. Should be just another week or two more of this, according to Dr. Thomas."

Emma swallowed uneasily, wondering what caused the sudden tightness in her chest. "I suppose that plan might work." She thought for a moment. Something about the plan seemed wrong, but she could not put her finger on what. "Aunt Mary will miss you. She has enjoyed having a guest in the house." If nothing else, it gave her something to brag about with the ladies from church. No one else could boast so fine-looking a suitor for their niece!

"Did you just agree with me for once?" Henry smiled at her, showing a glint of straight white teeth. The strange ache in Emma's chest grew stronger. "I didn't think you knew how to do that."

"Well, you know what they say, even a broken clock is right twice a day." Emma spoke with a lightness that she did not feel at all. Indeed, just now the world seemed unexpectedly heavy. "It should not be surprising that sometimes you have a good idea. It was bound to happen eventually."

He could have taken offense at that, and another time he might have, but today he merely laughed. "I am sure it won't happen again anytime soon."

"Very likely not. In fact, I had better leave you now, lest we quarrel again." She hoped he could not see how hard she had to work to force herself to smile as they exchanged goodbyes.

Once again, she peered through the cracked-open door to make sure no one else was in sight. This late, all the servants should be asleep, but one never knew. She stalked quietly back to her room and locked the door behind her. She drew in a deep breath, wondering why her legs felt shaky. Just a little over a week left, he had said. Well, she knew what to do. Gather ye rosebuds while ye may, as the poet said.

The sun shone brightly the next day, and Emma decided to act on her decision. "I am going for a ride, but

I do not need a groom today," she explained to Aunt Mary.

"I don't like you riding alone," Aunt Mary began. "What if your horse bolts?" No doubt she was thinking about what had happened to Henry when Bastian ran away with him.

"I am not going to ride cross-country. I will stick to the lanes. I am just going to drop off some preserves at Mrs. Murphy's place." Aunt Mary would accept that, because she approved of Emma doing charitable work. And Mrs. Murphy's house lay on the way to Emma's real destination.

Emma did bring a basket of preserves to the Murphy house. She would have felt guilty about lying to Aunt Mary if she had not done so. But she did not stay and listen to Mrs. Murphy's long list of complaints about Mrs. Elcott's most recent visit. Mrs. Elcott had the unfortunate habit of bestowing tracts on those members of the congregation whom she deemed in need of conversion, and Mrs. Murphy, who was known to distill her own whiskey and sell it to supplement her meager income, came in for a large share of her visits.

Normally, Emma would have lingered to commiserate with the widow. Mrs. Murphy spoke loudly and volubly, but rather surprisingly, her emotions tended to be subdued and well-controlled, and Emma did not mind her company as much as she did that of some of the cottagers. Emma enjoyed spending time with the youngest of the Murphy children, too. They were all lively and inquisitive. On other visits, she had brought a few of her favorite children's books, though it was hard to find stories that were not too dry and moralistic.

But today she had another errand, and she could not

afford to linger here. Aunt Mary would worry if she stayed away later than expected. Fortunately, Grannie Tavistock lived less than a mile up the lane from the Murphy cottage. The way lay along pleasant rolling fields, bisected by dry stone fences and dotted with sheep or cattle. There were few clouds in the sky that day, and Emma was glad to have a hat and veil shielding her face from the sun.

Grannie Tavistock's house was larger than that of most crofters, with a second story. The barn was good-sized, too, and the barnyard bustled with chickens. Her son managed the farm, because Grannie Tavistock had other work to do. Everyone in this part of the North Riding knew her by reputation, at least. She had delivered most of the babies born in these parts over the last two decades, and being a strong, hale woman, she seemed likely to keep delivering them—with the help of an apprentice—for many more years.

The barnyard was quiet when Emma rode in, but she did not have to call for help. A lad who looked no more than twelve came out of the house to take her horse for her.

"I won't be but a minute," Emma promised. At least, she hoped her errand wouldn't take long. She had never before had cause to consult a midwife, though, and she might be wrong.

She knocked at the door, but the boy holding her horse told her, "Go on in, miss. She be in the kitchen."

"Thank you." Emma took a deep breath and entered the house.

The door opened not into an entryway or hall but into a comfortable front room that seemed to be used as a parlor. An open doorway led into a short corridor, and

Emma found the kitchen in the back of the house. Grannie Tavistock sat at the kitchen table, grinding something with a mortar and pestle. She looked up and smiled.

"What brings Miss Ainsworth t' my door?" She had only a light Yorkshire accent, which rather surprised Emma. She had expected to hear the strong country burr of most farmers.

Emma's shoulders slumped with disappointment. She had hoped Grannie Tavistock would not recognize her. But she supposed she must be the only young lady in the area who covered her face with a veil.

"You won't tell anyone I was here, will you?" she asked, suddenly anxious about gossip.

"I'm like a doctor," Grannie Ainsworth said. "I keep my patients' secrets. What do you need, then, that you come to me and not to the surgeon or apothecary?"

Emma cleared her throat. "I need a contraception charm."

Grannie Tavistock's eyebrows shot up. "And what would you be needin' that for?"

Emma's face turned scarlet. What kind of question was that? "For the usual reason," she said stiffly. "Because I do not want to fall pregnant."

"I thought you were betrothed to the handsome young man who be stayin' up at the hall. Is that not so?"

"It is so." For once, Emma felt relieved that gossip had come so far. "That is why I need the charm, of course. We are to be married, and…and…"

"Does he not want an heir?" Grannie Tavistock had been grinding the herbs in the pestle the whole time, but now she set it aside and wiped her hands on her apron. She studied Emma closely. "Most men want to get their wives with child when they first marry," she said bluntly. "Brides come to me for fertility charms, but rarely for contraception charms." She smiled wryly. "Not until they have a few bairns already."

Emma gulped. Clearly, she had not thought this matter through all the way. She had not expected to be interrogated about why she needed the charm. "My fiancé has"—she cast her mind about for an excuse—"financial difficulties."

Grannie Tavistock snorted. "Westwinds and your fortune are not enough for him?" She arched her eyebrows. It was a fair point. One need not look into the account books to see that Westwinds was thriving.

"Look," Emma blurted out, "I can't tell you why I need it. But I do. Will you sell me one or not?"

She held her breath. If the midwife turned her down, she was not sure where she would go next. An apothecary shop might also sell preventive charms, but it would be far more public than Grannie Tavistock's house. Anyone might see her or overhear her. And she could not ask a maid to buy such a charm for her, not without fanning the fires of the gossip at the hall.

"Aye, miss," the old woman said. "I'll sell you one. When all is said and done, it isn't my place to judge whether you need it." She went to a wooden dresser and opened a drawer, pulled out a cloth bag, and took something small from it. She returned to Emma, but before she handed the object over, she said, "Whatever you're up to, I hope you take care of your heart as well as your body."

"My heart has nothing to do with this." Emma held her hand out to accept the charm. It was a piece of hardwood carved in the shape of a heart, with a hole bored through the top. She blinked in surprise at the shape, which seemed to ironically contrast with what she had just said. "What do I do with it?" she asked practically.

"You wear it," Grannie Tavistock explained. "Put it on a ribbon or chain and wear it like a necklace. Mind, you must keep it on when you go to bed with a man. It doesn't work unless you're wearing it. And it won't last forever. I'm a sorceress, not a witch, and sorcery doesn't last as long as wizardry or witchcraft. You either need to replace it after three months, or have a magician renew the spell on it."

"I won't need it longer than that." She would only need it for the next week or two. And she wouldn't need it at all if Mr. Dawson—*Henry*—continued to be stubborn. But she knew now that he desired her. All she had to do was convince him to act on his desires.

Chapter Fifteen

"You got *what*?" Henry hoped he had misheard. But he knew in his heart there was no mistake. He had very good hearing, and Emma had a clear speaking voice.

"I bought a contraception charm." Emma tilted her chin up boldly. As always, she was ready for a fight. "Now you need not worry about getting me with child."

"I wasn't worried about that, since we are not going to do anything remotely likely to make a baby."

Henry looked out the window for a moment, trying to figure out how to convince her that what she wanted simply would not happen. Not now, not ever. No matter how much he might enjoy it. He looked back at Emma, making the mistake of meeting her gaze.

She pounced. "But we already did do something remotely like it. You kissed me."

Henry rolled his eyes at this nonsense. "If you think you can get pregnant from kissing, Mrs. Elcott clearly did not do a good job of explaining things to you."

"You said *remotely*. Kissing certainly is remotely related to…" She paused and glanced away.

"Shagging?" he suggested, not liking to say anything cruder than that.

"Must you be so vulgar?" She wrinkled her nose at him.

"Yes, I must. If you can't stand hearing me talk about it, you certainly ought not to be doing it." He felt proud of himself for thinking of that. Really, a girl who blushed anytime he said anything about coupling ought not be trying to get into bed with him. Or anyone else, for that matter.

Though, eventually, she would have to marry someone, since her uncle was unlikely to give up his matchmaking on her behalf. That meant that someone else would get to—but he shied away from that unpleasant thought, closing the door firmly on it.

"In any case, you promised." She crossed her arms in front of her chest and frowned.

"I most certainly did not!"

"It was an implicit promise," she explained.

Henry shook his head. He wanted to pull handfuls of his hair out. He couldn't remember exactly what he had said yesterday. He knew, though, he had made no such promise.

"Emma," he began. But he had no idea what to say next. What was there to say that he hadn't already said? "This is a terrible idea."

"But you want to do it, don't you? And I want to do it. And everyone in the house thinks we're already doing it, so you need not worry about damaging my reputation." She ticked the arguments off on her fingers. "I have a charm, so you need not worry about illegitimate children. And," he heard her draw a deep breath, "Really, it almost seems like fate, doesn't it?"

"Fate?" Henry stared at her, having no idea what she was going on about now.

"I mean, that you should be stuck here, when you happen to be one of the few men I've met who could shield your emotions from me so well," she explained. "It's almost as if it were meant to be."

"Is that what you're telling yourself?" Henry felt equal parts fascination and horror. "You think God dumped me in your lap so you could experiment with me?" Thinking about her lap was a mistake, though; he realized that at once.

"I didn't say that." She waved her hand dismissively. Then she looked at him, her dark eyes beseeching him. "Please, Henry? There is no one else of whom I could ask such a thing."

Henry gulped. He turned and looked out the window. "If your uncle finds out I've ruined you and then abandoned you, he will kill me. Or have me before the court in breach of promise. And he would be well within his rights to do so." He sighed and shook his head, still refusing to meet her eyes. "Emma, don't you see you are asking me to behave like an utter cad? I can't do that."

"I am only asking you to act as my friend." Her voice quavered.

"Oh, for heaven's sake, don't *cry*!" Henry exclaimed.

He could not stand making her miserable. That was going to be his downfall, wasn't it? He could see no path that would not leave her miserable, one way or another, whether now or later. Was that the sound of her sniffling? Oh, that was unfair of her! He turned to look at her again. Yes, she was crying.

"Stop that!" he ordered. Which made her cry harder. "Look, just come sit with me." She crawled onto the bed with him, and he pulled her close to his chest. He was getting entirely too used to the feel of her body in his arms, the scent of lavender, and the way she sighed as she leaned against him. "You are going to be the death of me."

"I suppose I am terrible for asking such a thing of you," she muttered, speaking into his chest. "I must be shameless."

If there was anything worse than her tears, it was her self-loathing. Henry could not stand that. "You are not shameless," he admitted. "You have a perfectly good reason for what you want. Perhaps I am the one at fault." He knew, as soon as he said the words, that the argument was over and he had lost.

But although Henry could see defeat on the horizon, he saw no reason to admit that just yet. He suspected that if he agreed to do as Emma wanted, she would want him to do it *now*. She did not strike him as being particularly patient. He, on the other hand, was perfectly willing to take his time. Who knew when he would again have a beautiful girl in his bed? For all he knew, such a thing might never happen again. Besides, merely holding Emma in his arms was a pleasure, one he would have to forego once his leg healed and he left Westwinds. He might as well make the most of it.

So, rather than eagerly exploring the body that rested so enticingly close to him, he simply reached out to tug at one of the ringlets hanging beside her face. He longed to take her hairpins out so he could run a hand through her hair, but he did not quite feel bold enough to do so.

When Emma looked up at him, her eyes puffy with tears, he bent his head down and kissed her eyes. She shifted her head, tilting her chin up, so she could kiss him back, pressing her lips lightly against his. Yesterday such soft, gentle kisses had satisfied Henry. Today, they did not feel like enough. He let his mouth linger on hers, teasing her lower lip until she pulled away.

"Henry?" she said doubtfully.

"Emma," he murmured back, and kissed her neck, just below the ear. He felt her shiver in his arms, and he could not keep from smiling. So much for her attempt to seduce him! She was as skittish as a fawn when he touched her. Did she really think she could carry her plan out? "I think you ought to go back to your room," he advised. "It is getting late."

She looked up at him and rubbed her eyes like a sleepy child. "I am coming back tomorrow." Her words sounded more like a threat than a promise.

"Someone is going to catch you sneaking out of my room," he reminded her. It was all very well for her to say that didn't matter, since the servants already thought the two of them were misbehaving, but she would have to live with her ruined reputation after he left. He suspected she would find it uncomfortable to live in a house where the servants did not respect her.

But Emma merely shrugged as she got to her feet and tried to smooth out her crumpled dress. "Everyone thinks we are getting married in a few weeks anyway."

"It's what they're going to say when I'm gone that I worry about." He would never be able to show his face in this part of the county again.

And what about Emma? She would be forever known as the girl who had been ruined and then jilted by a cad. But if her only alternative was to be married to a fortune hunter whose father had died in disgrace, was that any better? Henry sighed. He wished he were clever enough to think of a better solution. Emma deserved better than either of those fates, and he did not know how to give her what she deserved.

He kept thinking about it after she left, leaving him alone with nothing but his doubts and frustrations for company. For a moment, he let himself imagine what life could have been like had Emma not been an heiress. Suppose she had been as poor as Henry? Everything would have been different then. She would have had to work for a living, as a seamstress or some such thing. Whatever it was that impoverished ladies did.

He could not picture Emma as a governess or companion. Living in a household with strangers would have been hard for her, given her empathy. But perhaps she could have taken in sewing or hat-making or something. She had a good sense of taste, so she might have done well at such work.

And he could have married her then, he thought wistfully. There would have been no discrepancy of fortune keeping them apart. Neither of them would have had any pride to be injured by an unequal match if they were truly equals instead. They would have lived in a single room with only the hob and the hearth for cooking, but the Emma of his imagination knew how to cook simple meals, however unlikely that might be in reality.

This being a fantasy rather than reality, he let himself imagine that his mother was self-reliant and his siblings grown, not needing his support, so he could keep all his pay for himself. Or, rather, he would give it all to Emma, and she would manage it for them very frugally.

They would have been poor, and they would have struggled and possibly even hungered, but there might have been moments of joy, too. Thousands of working people married on salaries as slim as Henry's, or even slimmer. Why could not they have done the same? It would have been a hard life, but better than the life Henry led alone in York, because he would have had Emma. Even toasted cheese would taste better with good company.

Henry let himself dream of that for a little while longer, and then he laughed silently to himself. That was his life, not Emma's. She had been born the heiress of Westwinds, and she would eventually marry some man who could bring her more than a tarnished family name and a passel of dependent relatives. She would probably have many children—he hoped she could teach them how to shield their minds at an early age—and she would certainly never have to toast cheese over an open fire for her dinner. When Henry went back to that life, he would go back alone.

Chapter Sixteen

The next night, Emma came to Henry's room wearing only a nightdress and a dressing gown. When he saw her, he scowled at her. But he did not order her out of the room, as she half expected him to do. Instead, when she sat down on the side of the bed, he caught her in his arms and kissed her fiercely, nipping gently at her lower lip as if he were a playful puppy.

"You are an idiot," he growled. "You should not be here."

"But I am here." Emma's heart executed some bizarre gymnastics in her chest that nearly distracted her from the warmth of Henry's hands on her waist and the taste of him on her mouth. Nearly, but not quite. His cologne smelled stronger than usual, and she wondered if he had put it on freshly just for her. That made her heart pound more heavily. "Please, Henry?"

"Please, what?" he teased her, looking down at her, an unfathomable expression in eyes that were bluer than the ocean. Even sitting on his lap, with his hands on either side of her waist, she could not get a reading on his emotions at all. "You can't say it, can you?" He shook his head at her.

Emma's face heated up. She swallowed nervously. He was right. Now that she was here in his arms again, she did not know how to ask for what she wanted. "Please, will you...can I...I want you so much! Please, can I have you?"

He slipped one arm around her, pulling her closer. "You are so persistent I don't see how anyone ever refuses you anything," he grumbled. That was not an answer. But he lowered his head and kissed her again, and this time his hand slid up from her waist to cup her breast. Emma caught her breath in surprise at the touch.

He pulled his head back from hers. "There are some things you can't undo once you've done them."

"I know," she whispered.

She had certainly considered that. In the eyes of society, she would be a fallen woman after this, no better than a streetwalker. Probably no one would ever want to marry her. But since it was not likely anyone ever would want to marry her except for the sake of her fortune, she did not see that it mattered much.

In Henry's eyes, she might be beautiful, but that beauty did not really belong to her. It was some trick of Henry's mind that made her seem so. Or perhaps some magic. He was a sorcerer, after all, so maybe it was no wonder he could make her feel beautiful. That enchantment would end when he left her, but why shouldn't she enjoy it for now? If she were honest with herself, it was not merely curiosity that drove her to his bed. She desired *him*. What woman *wouldn't* want to have Henry Dawson?

"I know the cost, but I still want this. If," she said shyly, "you want me." The magic would not work unless he desired her.

"Of course I want you." He spoke in a rumbling whisper, right in her ear, that sent goosebumps all over her skin. When he took her earlobe gently between his teeth, a shiver shook her, and her whole body flushed with heat. "And I am going to have you, just this once. That will be enough to remember."

"Remember?" Emma repeated, a little puzzled.

Instead of answering her, he kissed her again, and she forgot the question she had meant to ask him. All her attention was taken up by figuring out how to kiss. She had not realized before that tongues could be involved. She hoped she tasted of nothing worse than tooth powder.

But when Henry started to take her nightdress off, she stopped worrying about tooth powder. "No!" she whispered fiercely.

"You changed your mind?" He sounded puzzled. And perhaps disappointed, though that might have been her imagination.

"I did not change my mind!" Emma hissed. "But I want to leave my nightdress on." He stared at her, pulling his brows together thoughtfully. "I am not wearing any drawers underneath," she admitted, blushing. "So you can still…I mean…there is no need for you to undress me." She hoped he understood what she meant.

"But I want to see you!" He gently stroked her cheek. "I know you are beautiful. Please, will you show me?"

Emma shook her head. She was sorry to disappoint him—and she could see now that he was indeed disappointed—but she felt certain about this. The smallpox scarring was not as heavy on her torso as it was on her face, but she still did not want him to see her unclothed.

"Very well," he said. "But *I* am taking off my nightshirt, unless you object."

Emma's mouth went dry. She certainly did not

object. She had wondered what he looked like under his shirt. He had lost some muscle mass from being bedbound, though she knew he tried to keep active by doing stretches and exercises in bed. Even so, he looked incredible unclothed, a combination of angles and planes that fascinated her.

Feeling both shy and curious, she reached out tentatively to stroke his chest. Then her eyes wandered down his abdomen to his lap. When she realized that all that separated her from his lower body was a thin sheet—because he did not have drawers on, either—she quickly glanced up again.

"Don't be so shy," he told her, sounding amused. "You are going to be intimately acquainted with John Thomas, aren't you?"

"It has a name?" she gasped, and he laughed.

"I suppose you're going to tell me that girls do not give slang names to their body parts?"

Emma glared at him, but that only made him laugh again. "Not the girls I know!"

But really, when was the last time she'd had a private conversation with a girl her own age? Aunt Mary's sewing circle from church did not count. Emma had to choke back a giggle as she tried to imagine that group of charitable ladies discussing vulgar names for their anatomy.

"Men are disgusting," she concluded, wrinkling her nose at him.

"You are free to leave at any time, if my crudeness disgusts you," Henry retorted. "I think you know where the door is."

But as he still had one arm wrapped around her waist, it would have been hard for her to leave. Emma briefly wished she could box his ears for his impertinence. Since they were not children, and adults did not express themselves through violence, she simply pulled his head down so she could kiss him. That was more satisfying anyway.

While she kissed him, Henry slipped his hand under her nightdress so he could caress her thigh. Then his hand kept moving upward, and Emma's heart began behaving erratically again because she knew where that hand was going.

Henry pulled his mouth away from hers long enough to ask, "Is this all right?"

"Yes," she whispered, though she could not help tensing a little. No one had ever touched her there but herself, and even that she had not done often.

And, she quickly found, being touched by someone else felt very different from exploring her own body. In some ways it was frustrating, because she could not easily direct him the way she wanted, and she had no idea what he meant to do next. Then again, it could be quite pleasant to be surprised by a movement she had never expected. He could do quite interesting things by moving his thumb back and forth, for example. Emma leaned her head against Henry's chest and began to rock back and forth as she felt the tension between her legs growing.

"You like this?" he murmured in her ear.

"Yes! Please don't stop!"

The motion of his thumb back and forth over that sensitive spot seemed like the most important thing in the world, though Emma could not have said why. Then she gasped, as pulsing waves broke over her. Muscles she did not know she had spasmed to an unfamiliar rhythm. She heard herself moaning, though she had not intended to make a sound at all. But she could not seem to help herself. The shuddering sensation jerked the sound from her. It ended far too soon.

"Stop!" she hissed, because she no longer needed or wanted the motion of his hand. She clung to him, breathing heavily, as she tried to sort out what had happened. She had read enough of the more inappropriate books in the library to guess. "Did I just come?"

"I certainly hope so," Henry said, "because I think I might have sprained my hand doing that. I would hate to have to do that all over again." She could not see his face, but she could hear the smile in his voice.

She smiled back, though he could not see it because her face was buried against his chest. "Do shut up," she said affectionately. She tipped her head back so she could kiss him, thinking that his mouth might be better occupied that way.

She could feel him fumbling around with the bedclothes underneath her, but it took a moment to realize that he had pulled away the sheet separating her from his…well, she was not going to think of it as "John Thomas," so she supposed she might as well say "member." Torn between curiosity and embarrassment, Emma looked down. She felt her eyes widen. Was that thing actually going to fit inside her? If so, it must hurt like the devil! She gulped.

"You know," Henry whispered, "if you are not comfortable with this, we can stop here." He brushed his lips against her forehead and gave her a chance to think.

"No. I do not want to stop."

She needed to know whether her empathy would allow her to go to bed with a man, and the only way she knew of finding that out was to try it. But, beyond that, she wanted *Henry*. She had smelled him, tasted him, and touched him, and that was somehow not enough. She wanted more of him.

"How do we do this?" she wondered. "Do we have to lie down?"

Henry shrugged. "We could, but I don't think we need to. Why don't I just stay sitting, and you sit on my lap? Lower yourself down onto me. I will help you."

Emma nodded. He helped guide himself into her body as she slowly lowered into place. She had expected this part to hurt, but it did not. Perhaps taking things slowly helped. Apparently, he was not too big to fit. She sat with her legs folded, thinking her thigh muscles might protest this position if she stayed here for very long.

"Are you all right? Does it hurt?" Henry asked her anxiously.

Emma shook her head. "It does not hurt at all." She still found it all a little strange.

This close to Henry, it was hard to look him in the eyes—her head was at the level of his chest. She could smell the musky scent of his body combined with his cologne and a faint smell of soap. She rested her head on his chest, where she could hear his heart beating, racing. But she still could not sense his emotions or his sensations, even though they were so intimately joined. His mental shields were so good she would have to use words if she wanted to know what he thought.

"How does it feel to you?" she asked.

"Good," he said quietly. "I should warn you that I don't think I'm going to be able to last long."

"What do you mean?"

He kissed the top of her head before answering.

"This feels so good, even when you're just sitting still. I don't know what will happen if you start moving."

"I'm supposed to move?" Emma wrinkled her brow at the thought. How could she even move in this position, held tightly in his arms as she was?

Henry chuckled, tightened his arms around her, and rested his chin on her head for a moment. "Yes, you get to be in control. I am sure you'll like that."

She could hear a teasing note in his voice. She tilted her head back so she could look up at him and glare, but he only kissed her forehead again.

"I am sure whatever you do will be perfect." This time she could hear no hint of mockery in his voice. The warmth in his voice brought a blush to her cheeks, though she would have thought herself past the point of blushing now.

"So, what *am* I supposed to do?" she asked in a small voice. She hated that she did not know what to do or how to do it. There really ought to be better instructions for this sort of thing. Mrs. Elcott's hushed explanation of the marriage bed had not prepared her adequately. "How am I supposed to move?"

"Try moving up and down," he suggested.

Oh, of course. She felt silly for not having thought of that. It was easy enough to do, though Emma froze in shock when Henry moaned in pleasure.

"Don't stop," he begged, so she kept moving until his grip on her suddenly tightened and he groaned again.

And his mental shields, which he had always so rigorously kept locked against her mental touch, crumbled under the force of the pleasure that shook him. Emma, wrapped in his arms, her head resting on his chest, felt every pulse of his release just as he did. She whimpered and bit her lip, feeling shaken to the core on multiple levels.

If she had felt only his pleasure, that would have been one thing, but as he collected himself afterward, she caught a taste of his satiation, affection, concern, and guilt. She looked up, puzzled. What did he have to feel guilty about?

Chapter Seventeen

Henry tucked Emma's head under his chin for a moment, needing time and space to breathe after that. He wished he could stay like this forever, with Emma in his arms and nothing but a comfortable silence between them.

But there were things he had to say. "Emma, love, I am so very sorry." She moved her head back and looked up at him, and he knew from the look on her face that she was going to ask him what he felt sorry about. He clarified before she could ask. "I know I dropped my shields. I am sorry I wasn't able to keep them up."

"I suppose it was foolish of me to think you could, given the circumstances."

She sounded subdued, and he wished for a moment that he had some of her magic, so he could have some sense of what was going through her head. Did she already regret what they had done? Was she scared of the consequences if anyone found out? Or merely disappointed with how her "experiment" had failed?

"I guess it is good that you found that out now." He would have liked to bask in the warmth of their encounter, but that warmth was already fading, and a cold, heavy disappointment took its place. "We would never have worked together, would we?"

So much for his childish fantasies of sharing his life of poverty with Emma! He knew now they could never have had a life together, no matter what the financial circumstances. His mental shields were not strong enough to keep her safe. His heart ached with the knowledge that he could never be a proper husband to her.

"It does not matter," she said quietly. She leaned her head against his chest again. "I suppose I did not really have any idea what this would be like. All of my ideas were wrong." She sighed, then kissed his bare chest, almost absently. "Thank you for doing as I asked, Henry. I appreciate that."

Henry barely registered her thanks, because he was still puzzling over her earlier words. "Wrong in what way?"

She shrugged. He could feel the motion, since she still leaned against him. "I did not understand how...powerful...the sensation would be. Or what it would be like to share it with someone. I will have to think about it." Then, to his disappointment, she pulled out of his arms, slipped off the bed, and stretched. "I will see you tomorrow." Her voice sounded surprisingly formal, given how intimate they had just been.

Henry frowned. Surely there were more things to say than that? As she turned to go, he grabbed her hand. "Emma, are you really well? Is everything all right?" Had he hurt her—if not physically, emotionally? Hurting Emma was the last thing he wanted to do.

Emma turned back to him and smiled, though her smile wavered a little. "I am well enough, Henry. I just need some time alone."

He let her go, though he still worried about her. After the door shut behind her, he moved the bolster that propped him up, so he could lie down. The hour had grown late, and he felt tired, but he could not stop thinking. Taking Emma to bed had clearly been a colossal mistake, and he did not understand how or why he had let Emma talk him into it. He was older than she was (if only by a few years), so he ought to have been more responsible.

Henry sighed and covered his face with his hands, wishing he could hide from the consequences of his actions forever. Wishing he could just die of heartbreak, as his father had done. But he felt very much alive at the moment, and he knew better than to dodge his responsibilities.

He had deflowered Emma, ruining her in the eyes of the world. How could he simply run away and leave her? That could not be right. But to entrap her into a marriage with him could not be right, either. He would be the only one to benefit from such a marriage. He would restore his fortune and his place in society, but what would Emma gain? He might help salvage her reputation, true, but that was it.

If he could not shield his mind from Emma in bed, he could not even give her the children she wanted. It would have been bad enough to have married her before, when he thought he at least had something to offer in exchange for her fortune. To do so now, after learning that he could not be a true husband to her, would be downright criminal.

The last time Henry had cried had been when he found his father's body in the study at Switherton. He had always been relieved that he had been the one to find it, rather than his mother or—God forbid!—one of his siblings.

Still, it had been a shock. He had not yet known the

extent of his father's debts, and he had gone to the room expecting to talk to his father about what they could do to recover their fortune. Henry had believed that it would be only a matter of tightening their belts, selling off their hunters, and giving up luxurious dinner parties for a few years. He had had no idea how radically his life would change.

But the sight of his father's cold and lifeless body, still slumped over the desk, had shaken him to the core. Even before he understood how awful the financial situation really was, he realized that a door had been shut on his childhood forever. Once he ascertained that his father was beyond the hope of revival, he collapsed on the floor and burst into tears for the last time in his life. He only rang for a servant once he had wiped his face clean and gotten himself back under control. Even then, he had known that he would have to be strong for the rest of the family.

At least, he had thought it would be the last time he cried. But tonight, tears prickled at the edges of his eyelids, and his throat tightened with sobs that he did not want to release. He knew he would have to be strong again, and he was so very tired of that. He was tired of working and scrimping so his siblings might someday have a chance at a life he would never see for himself. When would he ever be allowed to have something all his own? He could not have Switherton back; he knew that. He could not have his old place in society. And now he could not have Emma. He was not good enough for her.

When he looked at where he stood in life, he was appalled at how wrong everything had gone. The young men Henry had gone to university with had earned their degrees and begun their lives. Some of them had begun reading law, studying medicine, or working as curates. Other eldest sons—those whose fathers had not made unfortunate business decisions—had gone home to learn to manage estates.

And the wealthiest of his friends were living lives of luxury, hobnobbing with the elite during the Season, visiting watering places in the summer, and shooting partridges or riding to hounds in the autumn. Soon enough, they would begin making advantageous marriages, either securing new fortunes for the next generation or increasing their family's riches and prestige.

Meanwhile, Henry had only made a deeper mess of the wreckage of his life. He had quit what was probably the best chance he had for a long-term career, in the hope of winning an heiress's heart. He had thought this was his chance to go back to the life for which he had been raised and educated. Instead, he had ruined everything.

Instead of showing up with a fortune to impress his family, he would have nothing to show for his summer but a broken leg, a broken heart, and, probably, a pair of crutches. He had deflowered an innocent girl, and now he saw no option but to flee in disgrace. He could not even do right by Emma. Instead of making her happy, he might have just ruined her position in society.

Was this what utter failure felt like? Was this what Henry's father had felt like before the heart attack that carried him so suddenly away? Henry rather wished his own heart would fail him, too, so that he would not have to pick up the pieces of his life and go on without Emma. But he was young and healthy and his heart pounded steadily in his chest, refusing to end his mental pain.

So he would have to keep going. Tomorrow, he would think about what to do next. Tomorrow, he would think about how he might escape Elwood Ainsworth's wrath and find a new position. He could not go back to York and his job at MacGregor's apothecary shop. That was over. But despite Emma's warning about Uncle Elwood's connections all over England, Henry thought he might find work somewhere else. He had taken no university degree, but he had been well-educated. Perhaps he could find work as a clerk or secretary somewhere. He at least had good handwriting.

Or, being a sorcerer, he might turn his magical talents to his benefit again. He had nearly two years of experience working in an apothecary shop now, which might count for something. There were plenty of other apothecaries in Yorkshire. Most towns of any size boasted one. Surely one of them would need an assistant?

Tomorrow, Henry would figure it out. For tonight, though, he let tears seep out from under his eyelids, crying silently for all the things he wanted and could not have.

Chapter Eighteen

Emma woke up the next morning and looked at her bedroom with critical eyes again. What was she doing here in this room that had been decorated for a child? She was the mistress of Westwinds. She was a grown woman. And she was Henry Dawson's lover. It was long past time to make some changes.

She dressed herself, then rang for Hattie. "Please help me with my hair today," she said to her maid. "And later, I would like you to remove the dollhouse from my room."

"Remove the dollhouse?" Hattie repeated, sounding surprised. The dollhouse had stood in that corner for more than ten years, after all.

"I have no use for it."

"Shall I have someone put it in the attic, then, miss?" Hattie suggested.

Emma considered that for a moment. Then she shook her head. "Put it in the nursery and have a drop cloth placed over it." It would be safer there than in the attic, where there were sometimes rats the gardener's terrier could not catch. And if the dollhouse ever were wanted again, it would be wanted in the nursery, wouldn't it? "You can have these bedcurtains taken down, too."

Once she had thought the lacy bedcurtains to be the height of elegance. Now they seemed rather frippery.

This room would probably not be hers much longer, but she might as well begin putting it in better order, in case it was ever needed as a guest room.

She still had redecorating on her mind when she came down to breakfast. "Aunt Mary," she said, without any preamble, "did you decide what color to repaper my mother's old room?"

"Oh, curious about that now, are you? You would not listen at all when I tried to talk to you about it last week," her aunt scolded.

"I am sorry," Emma said, and she was.

Aunt Mary and Uncle Elwood had been working behind the scenes to get her affairs in order, and all she had done was try to think of how to undermine their plans. She had ignored any marriage-related talk as much as possible, being certain the wedding would never come to pass. Now she saw that had been rather rude of her, if not downright ungrateful.

"What did you have planned for the master suite?" she asked.

"I was going to put in a pattern with roses, like what you have in your room. You have always been fond of roses." Aunt Mary smiled a rather sentimental smile. Perhaps it only seemed that way because Emma could sense her aunt's fondness and nostalgia. Aunt Mary bubbled over with affection this morning.

"Don't you think that color is rather childish, though?" Emma suggested. She said it gently, not wanting to hurt her aunt's feelings. But she was very glad they were having this talk now, before the room had been repapered. "I am tired of rose. What about something…" She frowned and cast about mentally for alternatives. Yellow? Red? Green? "What about something blue?"

She took a bite of her toast as she thought about that. "Do they make wallpaper in a Blue Willow pattern? I would like something like that. Blue and white."

"And what about the master's room?" Aunt Mary asked.

Emma could pick up on a touch of embarrassment now. Her aunt felt uncomfortable alluding to the fact that Emma would be sharing the suite with a man. Really, what a prude Aunt Mary was! Emma allowed herself a small smile of superiority.

"Do you know what color Mr. Dawson would prefer?" Aunt Mary prompted. "I asked him myself the other day, but he seemed not to know what he wanted."

"I will ask him," Emma promised. They needed to talk about many things, and that was rather low on the list, but perhaps she would get around to it eventually.

Last night, after her intimate encounter with Henry, Emma had lain in bed and tried to work through everything that had just happened. As she had told Henry, many of her preconceived notions about amorous congress had been overset by the actual experience.

What she had failed to consider when she worried about how her empathy might affect a marriage was that sensations and emotions a man was likely to broadcast in the throes of pleasure would not be negative ones. Even if Henry had been repulsed by her smallpox scars, it was unlikely that he would have been thinking about that at the moment of climax. And his shields were good enough to block out everything before that.

She had also not considered how her own body would react to the secondhand experience of her partner's sensations. Thanks to her empathy, Henry's release had triggered a second one of her own, which had been rather overwhelming. To experience her own pleasure on top of someone else's was almost too much.

She knew Henry had wanted her to linger in his arms afterward, and she had been sorry to disappoint him, but she had not lied when she said she needed time alone to think. And after she had some time to herself? Her conclusion had been that, strange and overwhelming as the experience had been, it had also been good. Perhaps when she grew more used to it, she would not find it so overpowering. But if not—so what? Loving Henry Dawson was worth a moment of disorientation.

What bothered her most, then, was Henry's reaction. She remembered very clearly what she had felt from him for that brief moment before he closed his shields again. He had felt guilty for what they had done. That broke her heart. She ought never to have persuaded him to do something he believed to be wrong. For her own part, she could not regret what they had done, but she did regret that she had badgered and begged Henry into something that violated his conscience. He had made it clear he did not intend to bed any woman but his wife.

Well, she saw only one way to help him adhere to that resolution. She must marry him after all. In her heart of hearts, she felt glad to have so good an excuse for doing so. Selfish though it might be, she did not want any other woman to have him.

After breakfast, she visited Henry. She found him plowing through the contents of a breakfast tray. Her eyes widened when she saw what he had been served. "Do you eat that much every day?"

He had a poached egg, just as she'd had, but he also had thick slices of ham and a tiny crock of preserves. No one had offered *her* ham! What had Henry done to get the kitchen staff on his side?

"In case you have not noticed, I am considerably larger than you are. Ergo, I eat more than you do. That should be no surprise." He gave her a belligerent look as he cut up the ham. "Don't worry, I will not be raiding your larder for much longer. Collins says that Dr. Thomas is to visit in a few days, and if he thinks the healing is going well, he will remove my cast. I will be out of your hair before long."

Emma's stomach plummeted. She glanced at the door, which she had left open a crack. No one was in the corridor just now, but a maid could walk by at any time. They would have to be quiet. She sat down on the bed next to Henry, ignoring the empty chair.

"Do you still plan to run away, then?" She silently prayed that he could be convinced to stay.

He looked up from his breakfast, frowning a little. "I think that would be best. Don't you?" He held her gaze earnestly. She was the one who looked away, not liking to meet the intensity in his eyes.

She had hoped that last night might have changed his plans. How foolish she had been! He had not wanted to bed her at all. He had only done it because she asked him to. Of course his plans had not changed. What right did she have to ask him to stay? He had made his intentions clear enough. If she had allowed herself to hope for something more than a single night, she had only herself to blame for her delusion.

Still, she could not let him go without protest. Her mouth felt dry and her heart pounded erratically, but she had to at least try to express herself. "I thought perhaps it would be best if we went along with the marriage." Her face began to heat up. "All things considered."

She hoped he would not ask what she meant by "things," because she was not sure she could explain herself. Clearly, they were not on the same page. She did not know what it would take to get him on her page. Perhaps she did not have the right to ask that of him.

"Is that what you want, Emma?" he asked softly.

She looked back and met his gaze again. He neither frowned nor scowled, but the lines of his face suggested that he felt troubled. "I think marrying would be the wisest course of action, yes. Under the circumstances."

Her heart ached, knowing this would not be enough to keep him by her side. But she did not know what would keep him there. If she burst into tears, flung herself into his arms, and begged him to marry her, he might give in. But she had her pride, didn't she? And it could not be right to trap him into a marriage he did not want. She cared too much about him to do that to him. Better that she live alone for the rest of her life, if it meant he was happier.

"Oh, Emma!" The tenderness and grief in his voice fractured her heart into a thousand pieces. "I wish I could be what you need me to be. I truly do, dear heart. But I can't. You saw that last night, didn't you?"

Emma had no idea what he meant, and she felt too ashamed to ask. "You were very good to me last night," she whispered. *She* had no regrets, but perhaps she should not be surprised that he did. "I am so sorry I cajoled you into doing something you thought wrong. You deserved better than that."

She remembered the conversation they'd had once about men's virtue, and she felt ashamed of herself for dismissing his opinion. Henry was a human being, not an object to be used. Perhaps, after all, she did not deserve him. Maybe his departure was her punishment for treating him so poorly. The lump in her throat grew larger.

"That is not what bothers me. I regret that I let you ruin yourself with me, that is all. But I am so sorry, love." He reached out and took her hand. She twined her fingers with his, appreciating that contact. "I wish I could see a better ending for us. I stayed up late last night, thinking. But I can think of no way that I can give you what you deserve. I think it best if I leave."

He brought her hand to his mouth and kissed it. Once, that would have seemed a very romantic gesture. After the intimacy of last night, though, this felt like a step backward into formality. Emma wanted to fling herself into his arms, cry on his shoulder, and tell him how much he meant to her. But he had made his wishes abundantly clear, and it would not be right to try to manipulate him again. Even so, her heart ached, knowing how deeply she could love him if he would let her.

She had to clear her throat before she could speak, as it had tightened from unshed tears. "I suppose you will go as soon as your leg is out of the cast?"

"As soon as I can," he agreed. "No point in prolonging the inevitable." He squeezed her fingers once more, then released her hand. "Whatever we may do when we go our separate ways, I will never forget you, Emma Ainsworth." He looked at her, his blue eyes open wide, and opened his mouth as if to say something else. Then he snapped his mouth closed and shook his head. Apparently, he had thought better of his words.

Emma felt beyond the power of speech. She nodded her head, then got up and left the room. She wandered out onto the grounds and flung herself on the small patch of lawn at the heart of the rose garden. The garden was in full bloom, and the scent of roses hung in the morning air. Aunt Mary was right about one thing—Emma had always loved roses. At first, the familiar smell comforted her. Then she wondered if the scent of roses would always remind her of her heartache now.

Because her heart was breaking. She recognized the feeling from when her parents had died of smallpox. This grief felt different, of course. Henry had not died. He would go on with his life somewhere else. Probably he would marry someone else. Maybe he would find another heiress to marry, one with whom he did not quarrel all the time. An attractive young man with his talents would land on his feet, one way or another. She knew she ought to wish him well. But that was hard to do, because Emma did not see how *she* was supposed to go on living without him.

Her uncle would, no doubt, keep finding suitors for her, and eventually she might even marry one of them, but whatever happiness she might find would be entirely different from the life she could have had with Henry. Emma and Henry would have fought like cats and dogs, yes, but they would have cooed like a pair of doves, too, some of the time.

Well, maybe. Maybe a marriage between them would have been like a union between two territorial tigers. But who was to say that tigers were unhappy together? Cats knew how to purr as well as growl, didn't they? Here, though, Emma's imagination faltered, as she had never seen a tiger in real life and had no idea whether or not they purred. She preferred to think they did.

She lay on the grass for nearly half an hour, waiting until the first paroxysm of grief faded. Then she got up and went back into the house, mentally listing all the things she would have to do. It was only after she left the garden that she remembered she had never asked Henry what color the master bedroom should be papered. It did not matter, since he was not staying to marry her. But she would have to make something up to tell Aunt Mary.

For some reason, that was the detail that made her break down and cry. She hid herself in a closet while she sobbed her heart out. Then she washed her face, straightened her dress, and went about the day's work. No one even noticed that she had cried.

A few days later, Dr. Thomas and Mr. Higgins, the local surgeon, met to confer over Henry's healing. Dr. Thomas believed that Henry's leg could come out of the cast, since he had been treated with the imported healing potion. Mr. Higgins insisted that it took no less than four months for a broken tibia to heal, and he refused to believe Henry's leg could be healed so soon, magic or no magic.

Emma was not surprised when Henry sided with Dr. Thomas and requested that his leg be taken out of the cast. At this juncture, she was peremptorily sent out of the room. Apparently young ladies were not supposed to watch medical procedures, even when they were being performed on supposed fiancés.

She lingered in the corridor, though, wanting to know the results. The wait seemed excruciating. Anxious as she felt to know what the doctors decided, she was not sure which outcome she preferred. If Henry's leg was still mending, he would have to stay at Westwinds for longer. That would mean more precious time with him. On the other hand, there might be advantages to making a clean, fast cut. The sooner he left, the sooner she could begin the business of healing her broken heart.

Mr. Higgins had poor control over his emotions, and Emma therefore knew the moment he admitted defeat. He felt a complicated mixture of amazement, disappointment, and discontent. It was not, she thought, that he wished ill on Henry, but he would like to have been right. Dr. Thomas, on the other hand, felt pleased on all accounts. He was happy for Henry, he was delighted that the potion had worked, and he was smugly content about having proven a surgeon wrong about a broken bone. The two gentlemen came out, still debating the case.

"Ah, Miss Ainsworth," Dr. Thomas said. "I am pleased to report that the leg has healed sufficiently that Mr. Dawson no longer needs a cast. Mr. Higgins here is going to send a pair of crutches around for Mr. Dawson's use. I have told your young man that he should walk no more than fifteen minutes at a time, a few times a day, for the first week. After so prolonged a period being bedbound, he will need to regain his strength slowly."

Emma nodded wisely, hoping that her face did not display the relief she felt. If he could only walk for fifteen minutes at a time, Henry could not leave Westwinds yet. She would have him for a little while longer, then.

She knocked on the door to the room, barely waiting for Henry's response to enter. He sat at the edge of the bed, stretching.

"It probably feels good to be able to move a little," Emma suggested.

He nodded. "And I can have a proper bath, by myself, instead of needing Collins' help to wash." The way he wrinkled his nose suggested how little he had enjoyed needing the attendance of a valet.

"But Dr. Thomas says it will take time for your body to regain its strength," Emma reminded him. "You shouldn't rush things." He shouldn't bolt out the door, just because his leg was out of the cast. She did not want him to hurt himself. And she did not want to lose him yet.

Henry rolled his eyes. "Yes, Mother. I promise to eat all my vegetables, too. And," he concluded piously, "I will say my prayers before I go to bed every night."

"See that you do." Emma spoke with a sternness she did not feel in the slightest.

She tripped lightly out of the room, relieved beyond measure to have Henry for a few more days. Or would it be a few more weeks? Likely it would take some time for him to grow strong enough to travel to wherever he intended to go. Being out of the cast was not the same as being fully recovered.

Later that day, as she watched Henry struggling to move with crutches up and down the corridor, she spun a happy fantasy in which he lingered at Westwinds to heal, only to end up falling in love with her, changing his mind about leaving, and staying there forever. It was a very pretty castle in the air, and it comforted her for a few days. It gave her the strength to continue chatting lightly with Aunt Mary about plans for the wedding.

The Monday after Henry was freed from the cast, Emma stood patiently while the seamstress had her try on some of her new clothes. Aunt Mary had the happy thought to dig out an ornate mantilla that her nephew, Emma's cousin Bertram, had sent her from Spain while serving under Wellington.

Emma tried the mantilla on while wearing her

wedding dress, and had to admit that the effect was stunning. She stared at herself in the mirror, torn between regret that she would not actually be able to wear this dress for a wedding and a ridiculous hope that perhaps somehow everything would all end happily. She could not help wondering what Henry would have thought of her in this ensemble.

Then, one week after Henry's leg came out of the cast, she woke up one morning and discovered he was gone. He had escaped in the night, taking his crutches with him. He left behind his trunk, presumably because he could not carry it himself. He left behind the leather purse of guineas Uncle Elwood had given him. And he left behind three sealed letters, one to Aunt Mary, one to Uncle Elwood, and one to Emma.

Aunt Mary sat at the breakfast table, crying while she read her letter. "Oh, Emma, I am so very sorry! I cannot believe Mr. Dawson would jilt you like this! We were all so mistaken in him!"

"It makes no matter."

Emma knew her words might not make sense, but she hardly knew how to string together a coherent collection of words. She had known Henry planned to leave, yes. But she could not believe he had left without saying goodbye. Without giving her one last chance to persuade him to stay. Without a goodbye kiss. She had expected an emotional farewell. They had, after all, been lovers, if only briefly. She had not expected to wake up and find him gone.

Perhaps the letter would explain, but she could not bear to read it in front of her aunt. She could not be certain of maintaining command over her expression if she did. She comforted her aunt while trying to force herself to eat some breakfast. Her crumpets and jam tasted like sawdust this morning, and she could only take a single bite of her poached egg. She forced herself to drink her entire cup of tea and gave up on everything else.

After breakfast, she took the letter to her room and unsealed it.

My Dearest Emma, Henry had written.

I must be a coward at heart after all, because I do not think I can bear to bid you farewell as I ought. You will probably not believe me when I say that I love you dearly and wish desperately that I thought it right to stay, but it is so. That is why I am leaving now, while I can, because if I stay any longer, I will simply grow to love you more. Perhaps it would be better for your sake if you could forget me, but I assure you that I will never forget you or this summer. Be well, my love.

Yours,

Henry.

Emma read this letter three times, her frown deepening with every reading. After the third time, she shook her head, folded the letter, and tucked it away in a drawer. My God, she thought, Henry Dawson was an *idiot*. How could he have left her like this if he loved her? She had no idea what delusion he labored under, but she could see that he was deluded. And now she was going to have to track him down so she could tell him that to his face.

Chapter Nineteen

For Henry, the trickiest part of making his escape was figuring out how to get to Whitby from Westwinds without anyone knowing. Walking or riding was out of the question, given the state of his injured leg. If he had known more people in the area, he might have arranged to hitch a ride with some farmer going to market—assuming there was a market day coming up. But he could think of no neighbors nearby whom he knew well enough to ask such a favor.

In the end, he had to dip into the purse Elwood Ainsworth had given him and bribe one of the grooms from Westwinds to drive him to Whitby after the rest of the household had fallen asleep. He used another coin from the purse to pay his stay at a coaching inn that night, and the next morning he caught a ride with a fellow guest bound for Scarborough. That part was easy enough. He had to make conversation with the solicitor who had kindly given him space in his gig, but Henry had always been good at conversing with strangers, and the journey took only a little over two hours.

He arrived at his family's row house, not far from St. Mary's church, while the morning air still smelled cool and fresh. He shook hands with Mr. Bond and invited him in for a cup of tea, but his new acquaintance was eager to continue on to his own home, so they bade farewell. Henry stood on the doorstep for a long moment, trying to gather his strength for the explanations he would have to make to his family.

He looked at the tall brick house with critical eyes. It had been built in the 1760s for a merchant and had later somehow come into the possession of the Fletcher family, though they were landed gentry. When his mother's father died, he left this house to his widow, Henry's Grandmother Fletcher. She lived there with only her lady's maid for companionship until Henry's mother moved in two years ago.

The house was in good condition, for his grandmother had a comfortable jointure. The street had become rather fashionable, being in easy walking distance of both the harbor and the church, so no one need be ashamed of the address. Even so, Henry wondered for a moment what Miss Ainsworth, heiress of Westwinds, would make of this little townhouse if ever she saw it. Not that there was any chance of that happening.

He opened the door and walked right in, not bothering to knock. This was his own home, after all, or as close to one as he had now. He did not need a servant to announce him. He put his valise down in the hall and leaned his crutches against the wall. He would not need them to limp the short distance into the drawing room.

"Henry! What in the world!"

As he had suspected, his grandmother sat in the most comfortable chair in the room, a book in her hand. She wore a black dress, as she had done every day for the last fifteen years, with a lace cap over her silver hair, and she looked like a piece of Henry's childhood that had been miraculously preserved despite the wreckage of his old life. He found himself smiling, regardless of his pain.

"Grandmother, don't get up. I will come to you." He walked over to her, stooped down, and kissed her cheek. "It is good to see you again." When was the last time he had visited her? Too long, he knew that.

"But my dear boy, you are hurt," she fussed. "Why are you limping? And you have lost so much weight!"

"Grandmother," he said, grinning affectionately, "give me a minute to sit down and rest, and I will tell you everything." Well, not everything, of course. He could hardly do that.

In fact, once he made himself comfortable in the chair across from his grandmother's, he told a very abbreviated version of the story, leaving Emma out of it entirely. He presented his stay at Westwinds as merely a chance to do some paid work in the library. He told his grandmother how much he regretted that his injury had prevented him from properly carrying out his task.

"It will take some time for my leg to heal completely. But I had better start looking for work now." He prayed she would not ask why he could not go back to the shop in York.

"You ought not start working again until you are in better shape," his grandmother said, shaking her head. "In fact, I wish you had stayed up at Cambridge, Henry. Have you ever thought of going back? Perhaps it is not too late to take your degree."

He sighed. "That is all over with, Grandmother," he said gently. "I need to find work."

Even if his grandmother had the funds to send him to university, which he doubted, he would rather she use that money for Jasper, instead. It was Henry's responsibility to make sure his younger siblings had a chance in life, and Jasper had considerable magical gifts.

He would need a good education to use them to advantage.

His grandmother peered up at him, her forehead wrinkled. "Henry, is there something else bothering you? You look unhappy."

"I am tired and in pain. That is all." Surely that was enough to account for his unhappiness?

The furrows on her brow deepened with concern, and he steeled himself for an interrogation. But just then his mother entered the room, and his conversation with his grandmother was completely derailed. His mother was shocked about his broken leg, horrified to learn that he had given up his position at the apothecary shop without having found long-term employment elsewhere, and anxious about the family finances.

"I don't know how I am going to pay my dressmaker, I really don't," she complained.

Henry rubbed his forehead and bit back all the retorts he longed to make. The only new clothes he had purchased in the last two years had been stockings, and only because his own were worn beyond hope of darning.

"Did you not make any money working at that manor house?" she asked.

"Not much. I spent most of the time in bed, you know."

He thought wistfully of the purse full of guineas Elwood Ainsworth had left for him. He could not touch that money. It had been given to him not as payment for his labor but as a gift to the prospective bridegroom. Since he was not going to marry Emma, he had no right to take that money. He had only taken a couple of guineas to cover his travel expenses, on the grounds that he had earned that much through his translation of the Ayles family spellbook.

"I will find work again, Mother." He tried to use his most reassuring voice, but it did not sound as convincing as he had hoped.

"You had better," she said, shaking her head. "Eliza has outgrown her old dresses, and we can let the hems down no further. Girls grow so quickly at that age, you know."

Henry nodded wisely and changed the subject, asking about his siblings' whereabouts. Jasper was out playing cricket with some local boys, and Eliza had gone to drink tea at another neighbor's house. Henry relaxed a little, feeling relieved they were not here to listen to his explanations and excuses. His mother's anxious questions were bad enough. She alternated between worrying that he might have a permanent limp and worrying that he would not find work. Her fretfulness exhausted him, especially since he did not really have grounds on which to reassure her on these points.

When the younger members of the family came home, Eliza demanded to know why he had sent so few letters from Westwinds and Jasper was fascinated by Henry's crutches. He borrowed them and tried to hop up and down the hall, with rather disastrous results— possibly because they were too long for him. At sixteen, he did not have Henry's height. Henry suspected he might take after the Fletcher side of the family rather than the Dawsons. Eliza, on the other hand, was indeed growing like a weed. She was already as tall as Mother, and at twelve, she was likely to grow taller yet.

Henry wondered, for a painful moment, what would have happened if he and Emma had had children. Would they have been built like the Dawsons: tall, big-boned, with hands and feet that outgrew gloves and boots too quickly? Or would they have taken after Emma's family, who all seemed built on slighter lines? Not that Emma was small, exactly. She just seemed so because Henry himself was so overgrown.

But none of that mattered, he reminded himself. He and Emma could not have children together. He lacked the control over his emotions that she needed from a husband. Good as his ability to shield his mind might be, it was simply not adequate for Emma. And that was just as well, anyway, wasn't it? Emma deserved better than a fortune hunter who would fight with her every day of his life. He hoped that someday she found a husband who deserved her.

Henry tried to smile and nod as Eliza chattered about the girls' school she attended. But the concerned looks his grandmother kept giving him suggested that he failed to hide his real state of mind. His siblings' presence at least prevented Grandmother from asking any prying questions. He felt grateful for that.

At his mother's insistence, Henry spent the next few days resting at home. It was, in fact, both painful and tiring to walk about. As Dr. Thomas had warned him, his whole body was in poor condition, despite his attempts to do stretches and exercises while bedbound. He reluctantly faced the fact that he would not be able to find work immediately, as he had hoped. He still needed time to recuperate.

After two weeks of resting and taking short daily walks, he traded his crutches for a cane and betook himself to the only apothecary shop in town to see if the owner needed an assistant. That was the only field in which he had practical experience, and he had been reasonably good at his work. But he was out of luck. This apothecary had a son already in the trade and a young apprentice learning from them both. He certainly needed no assistant. This did not surprise Henry, but it disappointed him. He walked back home feeling both exhausted and despondent.

"Henry?" his grandmother called from the drawing room when he came in. "Where did you go?"

"Job hunting, but no sign of my quarry." He sank onto the sofa with relief and propped his foot up on an ottoman.

"I think you ought to consult Mr. Beverly," she suggested. "My solicitor. He might know of someone who needs a clerk."

"That is not a bad idea." Henry rather wished he had thought of that himself. "Thank you, Grandmother, I will do that." Maybe not until tomorrow, though. Or even next week. Leaving aside the crutches so soon might have been a mistake.

"My dear boy, I wish you would tell me what is really wrong."

"Really wrong?" he repeated, cocking his head to one side, as if she had puzzled him. "Isn't it obvious that my leg is still mending? It is only to be expected that it pains me still." He was, in fact, quite lucky to be out of bed so soon after a bad break. If not for that German formula, he would still be stuck at Westwinds. He ought not complain about a little pain and fatigue.

"I am not talking about the pain in your leg," his grandmother said. "I want to know what causes your heartache."

She looked across the tea table at him with knowing

eyes. He recognized that look from his childhood. It was the look he had earned when he ate a cookie from the cookie jar and then lied about it. His grandmother was very good at detecting truth from falsehood. She had a touch of sorcery, like Henry did, and he had always wondered if her ability to discern a lie was a magical gift.

Henry tried to laugh this off, but his laugh sounded fake even to him. "Oh, Grandmother, I cannot tell you about that."

"Why not?" She looked at him expectantly.

"It is not entirely my story to tell. It involves someone else…" He stopped, horrified by the realization that he had already given too much away.

His grandmother smiled. "I thought as much. A girl, then, Henry?"

Henry groaned and leaned his head back against the wall, closing his eyes. When it came to subjects like this, he had much rather talk to his mother than his grandmother. His grandmother had entirely too much perspicuity. His mother, though capable enough in her own way, would not have seen whatever it was his grandmother saw in his expression.

Still keeping his eyes closed, Henry weighed his options. He could not lie to Grandmother and hope to get away with it, but he could refuse to tell her anything. Or he could tell her an expurgated version of the story.

"There was a girl at Westwinds," he admitted. "I admired her very much." That was one way of putting it.

"But she did not care for you?" his grandmother suggested.

Henry shook his head. "I don't know what she thought of me." Other than the fact that she had thought him a good subject for her sexual experiments, that is.

For most of his stay at Westwinds, Henry had been under the impression that Emma did not particularly like him, though there were moments—he swallowed, thinking of the hurt on her face when he had told her he planned to leave—there had been moments toward the end when he had wondered if she cared about him a little. Not as much as he cared about her, obviously. But a little.

"It does not matter what she thought of me, Grandmother. The fact of the matter is that I was not good enough to aspire to her hand."

"You ought not say such nonsense," his grandmother said sharply. "*My* grandson would be good enough for a princess. If there were one your age available."

"Oh, Grandmother, you are the only one in the world who would think that!" Henry could not keep from grinning, though.

"I would like to know why you think you were not good enough." She frowned at him fiercely as she listed his assets. "You are the son of a gentleman, and you have been educated as such. You are hardworking and dutiful. I don't know why you think so little of yourself."

"Have you forgotten that I am penniless?" Henry reminded her. "I am the son of a gentleman, yes, but my father died in disgrace. I do not even have a respectable profession with which to support a family."

She sighed and shook her head. "Henry, I should not speak ill of your father, but you are twice the man he was. I daresay you take after the Fletchers rather than the Dawsons."

"Grandmother! You cannot speak that way to me of my father!" Henry spoke sharply, though some part of him wanted to laugh, too, at the old lady's partiality.

"It is the truth!" she insisted. "You have always been my favorite grandson, you know."

"Grandmother, I know for a fact that you say that to all of your grandsons." He had learned this from one of his cousins when he was thirteen. Before that, he had actually believed his grandmother when she said he was her favorite. But he had since learned that Jasper had heard the same. "We cannot *all* be your favorite."

"Yes, you can," she insisted illogically. "I would not lie to you all about something like that. And I wish you would listen to me on this matter, Henry."

"I am listening, Grandmother," he said patiently. "What is it that you think I should do?"

"I think you should go speak to Mr. Beverly about finding work as a clerk. And when you have a job again, I think you should go back to Westwinds and propose to this girl you are in love with. The worst that could happen is that she might reject you, after all."

Actually, Henry thought, the worst that could happen would be that Uncle Elwood shot him on sight for ruining Emma and then jilting her. But he could not explain that to his grandmother. She would be horrified if she knew he had bedded a genteel young lady to whom he was not married.

"And then," his grandmother continued, before he could ask how she thought a clerk could adequately support a wife, "You should bring her here. There is room enough in this house for another person."

Henry closed his eyes again and pictured that. It was a very pretty dream. Emma would get along well with his grandmother, he thought, if not his mother. She would surely find charitable causes for which she could sew blankets or knit scarves or whatever it was that she did with the women from church. She would keep busy with her charities while Henry worked, and at night he would come home and argue with her half the night.

And the other half of the night? Aye, there was the rub! He supposed they would just have to sleep side by side, feeling frustrated. Or at least he would be frustrated, since whatever he might do to please Emma, *he* would not be able to finish. What kind of marriage was that?

For the first time, it occurred to him that he might, given adequate practice, have gotten better at keeping his shields up. He had not been born with excellent mental shields. He had had to practice them because of his annoying friend. If he could improve his shields enough to keep Thompson out of his head, who was to say he could not improve them enough to protect Emma?

Why had he not thought of this before? He had accepted Emma's claim that their experiment was a "litmus test" that would show whether or not she ought to marry. But why had neither of them considered that more than one attempt was necessary to master most skills?

"You could be right, Grandmother. I might have made a mistake." A terrible, hurtful mistake. He felt sick to his stomach just thinking of it. He wanted to bury his hands in his face and groan in despair, but he knew that doing so would merely raise more questions.

"Well, then," she said briskly, "you had better figure out how to fix it, hadn't you?"

"If I can," he said doubtfully. As he had told Emma, there were some things that could not be undone. He very much feared that Emma Ainsworth hated him right now. There might be no way to mend the harm he had done.

Chapter Twenty

August 1814

Emma peered up at the narrow building doubtfully. She was not sure what she had expected, but she had not expected this. The ground floor of the rather sooty brick building was occupied by a cobbler's shop. The top floors contained "Rooms to Let," as a placard in the window proclaimed. One of those rooms was Henry's. Or at least it had been, a few months ago.

"I suppose we had better ask who rents out the rooms," she said to Hattie.

"Yes, miss." Hattie's face looked pinched and disgruntled. She had not wanted to come to York with Emma. She did not think Emma ought to be there at all, and she had accompanied Emma only because she thought it worse for Emma to go without an attendant.

Wealthy young ladies did not travel alone. That was for governesses and poor relations. An heiress must always have an attendant. It would have been better, in Hattie's opinion, if Emma had brought a manservant to attend her, but the Ainsworths did not keep a footman, and they were short a groom. Uncle Elwood had already dismissed the groom who helped Henry sneak out in the middle of the night, and he had yet to hire a replacement.

Emma entered the cobbler shop and shyly asked who let out the rooms above the shop.

"That would be Mrs. Brown," the cobbler told her. "You'll find her on the first story, first door on your left. She's likely in at this hour."

He was right, Mrs. Brown was at home. She opened the door readily enough and let Emma and Hattie into her cluttered front room. "You're looking for Mr. Dawson? Oh, I'm sorry, miss, but I've not seen him since May."

Emma nodded. She had expected that answer. "I hoped that perhaps he might have sent you a forwarding address?" Mrs. Brown narrowed her eyes. Emma easily read the suspicion she felt. "I need to contact him about some money that he is owed."

This was not a lie. Henry had left without collecting the full salary that Uncle Elwood had promised him, to say nothing of the two hundred pounds that he had apparently earned by staying at Westwinds for more than a month. Emma had had some harsh words to say to her uncle when she learned about *that* bargain. Henry had taken only about five pounds with him, as far as they could tell.

Uncle Elwood felt that goodbye was good riddance, and he seemed more inclined to sue Henry for breach of promise than pay him what he himself had promised. Emma, on the other hand, thought Henry deserved compensation for his broken leg. He had, after all, injured himself while accompanying her.

But of course Emma had other reasons to look for Henry. She needed to confront him, to demand an explanation of why he had run away if he really loved her. She needed to slap him in the face—or, if not that, at least tell him what she really thought of his cowardice, in such terms as he could not possibly misunderstand.

And then? Depending on his answer, she might need to kiss him. She had not made up her mind on that point yet.

"He did leave an address," Mrs. Brown said. "Let me see if I can find it."

Emma waited, tapping her foot, as Mrs. Brown shuffled about the flat, poking into various baskets of letters. She wished she could sweep in and search the woman's letters herself, because it seemed to take forever to find the requested information.

"Here it is. He sent me money to pay the rent for a whole month and said that I could just dispose of his things."

"Dispose of them?" Emma repeated, surprised. She would not have thought Henry could afford to give up any of his possessions.

Mrs. Brown shrugged. "Mr. Dawson thought it was not worth the cost of sending them to Scarborough. He did not leave anything of value behind, you know. Except for the books. He did want those." She looked up at Emma, suddenly hopeful. "Maybe you could take the books with you and deliver 'em to the young man? That would save shipping."

Emma smiled. Perfect! Now she had another excuse to track him down. "I could do that, but you must give me his address."

Her smile deepened as Mrs. Brown slowly copied out the address and handed it to Emma. She read it, feeling a mixture of surprise and delight. Scarborough! She could not believe he had run only that far away. Why, she could get there from Westwinds in just a couple of hours. This was perfect. She could go there tomorrow.

She reckoned without her relatives. When she left for York early that morning, she had told Aunt Mary she was only going into Whitby to visit a bookshop. Her aunt had been surprised, given how rarely Emma ventured into town, but pleased that Emma was getting out of the house. She had not been so pleased when she found the note Emma left for her, explaining her true errand. Emma had been certain her aunt would not want her going as far as York by herself, and she was right. Emma made it home just in time for dinner, only to discover that she was in the deepest trouble of her life.

"And the worst of it is," Aunt Mary said tearfully, "that I can't trust you anymore! To think that you would run away from home like that!"

"But I didn't run away!" Emma argued. "I merely went on an errand." An errand that took her more than four hours away from home, true. But she had returned as quickly as she could. "I used my own money to pay for the journey." She had had to change horses more than once, of course, but she could afford it. "You can see that I came back safe and sound. Harrison knows what he is doing."

"But you could have been killed! Or kidnapped! Or held up by highwaymen!"

None of these things seemed the least likely to Emma, but she could tell her aunt had been genuinely frightened by her absence. She wanted to reassure her aunt that she would not do it again, but she could not honestly say that, given that she planned to go to Scarborough as soon as she had the chance.

That chance did not come as soon as she expected it. The coachman, Harrison, was strictly forbidden to take her anywhere without her aunt's express permission, and when she tried to bribe him to take her to Scarborough, he shook his head and refused.

"It's as much as my position is worth to do that again, Miss Ainsworth." He spoke politely but firmly.

Emma would have to find another way to get to Henry. Perhaps she could ride to Scarborough, though it would be a long journey on horseback. And it had become difficult to get away from her aunt for very long. Aunt Mary had meant it when she said she no longer trusted her. Every time Emma took her mare for a ride, a groom accompanied her, even if she stayed on Ainsworth land. She found this very annoying, especially since she had just celebrated her twenty-first birthday. She was no longer a minor, but she was being treated like one, and she was not sure how she could get away.

She had yet to come up with a solution when the problem was taken out of her hands in a most unexpected way. She sat brushing her hair at her dressing table one night, preparing for bed, when something rattled against the window. Odd. It sounded almost like hailstones, but that could not be. She knew the sky was clear tonight, because she had seen the gibbous moon out the window earlier. Maybe a beetle flew into the window? She looked back into the mirror, but the sound came again, so she rose and walked to the window. Someone stood below her window, holding a mostly shuttered dark lantern.

Emma opened the window and looked out, squinting at the shadowy figure. "Who's there?"

"Can't you tell?" a very familiar voice said indignantly. "And you call yourself an empath!"

Emma's knees felt suddenly weak, and she had to

clutch at the windowsill to keep herself standing. "Henry," she hissed, mindful of the need to keep quiet. "What are you doing here?"

"I came to get you." He spoke casually, as if it were the most reasonable thing in the world. "So that we can run away together."

If he had had his mental shields as tightly locked as usual, she would have assumed he spoke in jest. But he stood before her without any psychic walls. She could tell he spoke in earnest. Also, he felt terribly, terribly anxious. He spoke boldly, but he half-expected to be rejected. Maybe more than half.

"Why would we run away?" Emma asked, stalling for time. She had spent many hours thinking about what she would say to Henry when she finally met him again, but she had not expected anything like this. All her plans were thrown off.

"Because I love you."

Because Henry's shields were still down, she could tell he meant what he said. That answered one of her questions, didn't it? Henry had written the truth when he wrote that he loved her. She closed her eyes, overcome by emotion—some of it hers, some of it his.

But Henry kept talking. "I want to marry you, Emma. For real, not in pretense. But I'm afraid your uncle will shoot me if I try to call on you in the time-honored fashion, so I really think it would be best if we get married before I have to see him again. He wouldn't want to be the one to make you a widow, you know."

Emma smiled. There might be some truth to what he said. Uncle Elwood was not a violent man, but he had been very angry with Henry for jilting her. He was not likely to encourage Henry's suit, not after the way Henry had run away. On the contrary, he would probably do anything in his power to keep Henry and Emma apart.

"You are an idiot, you know." Emma had imagined herself saying that many times, but she had never imagined how much affection would color her voice as she said it. "I ought not love you."

"You really shouldn't," Henry agreed. He meant that, too. He did not think he deserved her. "But I hope that you do, all the same. Because nothing would make me happier than to spend the rest of my life with you. Will you marry me, Emma Ainsworth?"

Emma wanted to smile broadly, but she forced herself to scowl. "I really think you ought to apologize first. The nerve of you, coming to propose to me after you ran off without saying goodbye!"

"I am very sorry," Henry said, though he seemed to be on the verge of laughter. He must know her well enough to tell she was not really angry at him. "But you know, I am getting a crick in my neck from looking up at the window. Why don't you pack a valise and sneak out of the house? I can make my apologies better when you are on the same level with me."

"Oh, all right," Emma said, trying to sound as if this were nothing out of the ordinary. Perhaps she ran off with handsome young men every day. "Just give me fifteen minutes to pack."

"Make it ten," he recommended. "I'm worried someone will see my chaise in the barnyard. I'd rather not get caught absconding with an heiress."

"I will hurry," Emma promised.

But packing a valise for an elopement was tricky. She needed her toiletries, of course, and underclothes, but which dresses should she pack? A walking dress, she supposed, but would she want an evening dress too? She hesitated, and, feeling foolish in the extreme, rolled her ridiculous wedding dress up, along with the Spanish veil, and tucked it into the valise.

She dressed in her best walking dress and crammed her nightgown into the valise. The bag was so full she could hardly snap it shut. Well, that would have to do. She put on the first bonnet she found and snuck out of her room, walking as quietly as she could. She remembered to avoid the creaking floorboard just before she reached the stairs. She took the servants' staircase, because that was the fastest way to get to the side door. The tightly bolted door squeaked a little when she opened it, but no one seemed to hear.

She shut the door behind her and looked for Henry, but he found her first. He swept her into a tight hug, pulling her off her feet and into his embrace. Emma buried her face in his topcoat and breathed in the smell of his musky cologne.

"What is that scent you wear, anyway?"

"It's called Cádiz," he said, laughing. "It was popular with undergraduates when I was up at Cambridge. I'm almost out of it, though. I'll have to find something cheaper."

"No!" Emma protested. He should never change his cologne. That scent would forever be associated in her mind with the strange month when she fell in love with him. "I will buy more for you. I have plenty of pocket money."

She stiffened, remembering that since she was one-and-twenty, she had control of her fortune now. She did not need Uncle Elwood's permission to sell out of the Funds or draw from her bank account.

"You should not spend your money on me," Henry scolded.

Emma tipped her head up, intending to explain how wrong he was, but before she could argue with him, he kissed her hungrily. She kissed him back just as fervently, reaching up and burying one hand in his hair as she licked his lower lip.

Then she remembered that he had not sufficiently repented. She pulled her mouth away from his, albeit reluctantly, and wriggled out of his embrace.

"Is something wrong, love?" he asked innocently. He had finally put his mental shields back up, which she found both comforting and frustrating.

"I ought to make you beg, after the way you treated me!"

Henry laughed. "Too late for that. You're already here, and I'm going to run away with you now." And, much to her surprise, he scooped her up in both arms, as if prepared to literally carry her away.

"At least say more than 'I'm sorry,'" Emma demanded. "You can do better than that." Henry was certainly capable of being articulate when he wanted to be.

"I am deeply, profoundly, absolutely stricken with remorse for my actions," Henry said glibly. "And I firmly intend to spend the rest of my life in atonement." It would have been a better apology if she could not feel his shoulders shaking with silent laughter.

"Say it like you mean it!"

"It," he said solemnly.

Emma closed her eyes and groaned audibly. "I could still run back into the house," she reminded him, "and wake up the household. Our butler knows how to shoot a gun, you know." Iverson had served as a batman in the army many years ago, though he always claimed to prefer butlering to soldiering.

"Emma," Henry said, "my leg hurts, and I need a strong cup of tea that I probably won't get until we reach Scarborough. I really think we had better leave now. We have the rest of our lives for me to spend groveling, if you like. But I do not want Iverson to shoot me."

"Scarborough?" Emme repeated, wrinkling her brow in confusion. "Aren't we running away to Scotland?" That was the traditional way to elope, wasn't it?

"Why would we do that when we could just get married in my parish church?" Henry wanted to know. He carried her away from the house, toward the barnyard. The waxing moon hung high in the sky, bright enough to illuminate their way.

"Because it takes time to get a license." Marrying by common license was much faster than calling the banns in church, but it still took time.

As Henry strode toward the barnyard, Emma wondered if she should offer to get down and walk. She could tell from his faint limp that Henry's leg had not fully healed. But before she could suggest that, he had reached the rented chaise, a standard Yellow Bounder with a single seat inside. A postboy idled by the carriage, illuminated by the carriage lanterns, but he stood to attention as Henry approached.

Henry put Emma down and opened the door so she could get in. He waited until Emma settled into the chaise to answer her.

"I got a license last week," he said cheerfully. "We could get married tomorrow if we want. Except that I'll probably need to sleep the whole day through to make up for tonight. The day after tomorrow would be better."

"Oh." That was rather presumptuous planning on Henry's part, given that he had not known Emma would say yes. Emma felt a tiny bit disappointed. It would have been fun to run off to Scotland with Henry.

"Of course," he said doubtfully, "if you really wish to go all the way to Scotland, we can. But it seems needlessly extravagant. And my grandmother wants to attend the wedding, you know."

That spoiled the effect even further. "It's not much of an elopement if your grandmother is in attendance." Few things could make a hasty wedding more respectable than someone's grandmother in the congregation.

"My siblings want to come, too. My sister has never attended a wedding before." Henry stood up and stepped back, no doubt intending to speak to the postboy about their departure.

Emma's heart thumped uneasily at the idea of meeting more people. "Er, will I meet your whole family?"

She tried to keep her voice cheerful and upbeat, rather than reveal how uneasy the idea made her. Meeting new people meant awkwardness and discovery. Would the new people react badly to her scarring? Would they have good control over their emotions, or be the sort who felt strongly and had no ability to keep their feelings to themselves? So many things could go wrong.

"Of course you'll meet them!" Henry spoke lightheartedly. Either he had not picked up on her uneasiness or he was trying to cheer her out of it. "That's where we're going, you know. To my grandmother's house in Scarborough. Normally, she lives with just my mother, but the children are still on holiday from school, so it's a bit crowded. But don't worry, there will be room for you!"

He turned on his heel and walked to the horses, whistling happily. Emma very nearly called after him to remind him that he ought to be quiet. But she would have had to raise her voice in order to do so, and that would have been ironically unhelpful.

Besides, she had other things to worry about. Surely Henry knew how uncomfortable it would be for her to live with strangers? But, she reminded herself, it would only be for a short time. After they were married, they could come back to Westwinds. Uncle Elwood would have to forgive Henry once Emma had married him. Or, if not forgive him, at least tolerate him. Otherwise, her uncle's visits to Westwinds would be terribly strained.

Then Emma realized that it would be up to her now whether Uncle Elwood was even allowed to visit his boyhood home. He was no longer her legal guardian. The house had not been entailed, and her grandfather had left it to her absolutely, since she was the only child of his eldest son. It would be terribly rude to refuse Uncle Elwood admittance to Westwinds, but if he did not accept Henry, she could do that. She would not have to admit any guests she did not like. She smiled at that thought.

Once she married, she would no longer need Aunt Mary to serve as either a guardian or a chaperone. It would be Emma's decision whether to keep her on as a companion or send her away. The very thought of so much power sent a shiver down her spine. She could donate more money to the children's hospital she patronized…

Except, she remembered, after she married Henry, she would no longer have control of her property. Thanks to the law of coverture, she would no longer be able to sign contracts or engage in legal dealings. Henry would control their property. It would essentially belong to him. She sat staring at her clasped hands as she considered that. She listened as Henry talked to the postboy. And she wondered what her married life would be like.

"It will take us a couple of hours to reach Scarborough," Henry warned her as he settled beside her.

Emma nodded. Then, realizing he might not be able to see her in the dark, she spoke. "Very well."

"Is something wrong?" Henry covered her hand with his own. "Having second thoughts?" He spoke in a voice barely above a whisper as the chaise began to move. "Do you want me to stop the carriage?"

Emma gulped. Did she? It was not too late to call the elopement off. She could marry Henry later, and in the meantime, have her fortune placed in settlement so he could not touch the capital. Once she was married, it would be too late to do that, wouldn't it? Emma grabbed Henry's hand and squeezed it tightly. Legally, he would have control of her, as well. Women were expected to obey their husbands.

"Henry, you do realize that when you marry me you will have complete control of my land and my fortune? What will you do with it?" Her heart pounded anxiously as she spoke.

"Leave it to you to manage," Henry said promptly. "I will have my own work to do, you know. I won't have time to manage your property for you. Though of course I should be happy to help if you need help. But I don't think you will. You know Westwinds better than anyone."

Emma relaxed a little. "I do, don't I?"

She leaned her head on Henry's shoulder, and he tucked an arm around her. He could, of course, be lying to her. Once they were married, he could do what he liked with her fortune and her property, just as he could legally do what he liked with her body. But Henry was not in the habit of lying. If anything, he was likely to speak the truth too bluntly.

Even so, it would be good to ask questions now. "And it will be for me to decide what we spend my money on?"

"Yes." He kissed the top of her head. "I do not want your money, Emma Ainsworth. I wouldn't touch it if you offered it to me. I want *you*."

Emma's lips curled up in an automatic smile. Her hands, which had felt cold and clammy from nervousness, seemed to warm up. Perhaps that was due to Henry's proximity. Or maybe it was that magic he had, the ability to make her feel beautiful, precious, and loved.

"You shall have me," she told him. "But mind, I will have *you*. And you cannot get away from me once you are mine. You must stay with me forever." Till death do us part, as the marriage ceremony said.

She thought these words sweet and moving, but Henry chuckled. "I am your captive, then? Very well, Miss Ainsworth. You have won. I am your obedient servant."

He rested his head on hers, and Emma was so happy she feared her heart might literally burst. Did people ever die of joy? She could remember many times when her heart had ached with sorrow or fear, but she could never remember aching with happiness as she did now.

She had to do something to stop that pain. She reached up in the darkness to find Henry's face and pulled it down to hers so she could kiss him. It was rather hard to find his mouth in the darkness, but they managed. Managed quite well, in fact.

Chapter Twenty-One

Grandmother Fletcher wanted to invite all her cronies from the neighborhood and her church to the wedding, but Henry gently rejected this proposal. One look at Emma's face when she heard the suggestion was enough to remind him of how she struggled with crowds. When they married, two days after running off from Westwinds, the congregation consisted solely of Henry's immediate family, his grandmother, and his grandmother's solicitor, Mr. Beverly.

The inclusion of the latter gentleman very much puzzled Henry. It became clearer when, as he signed the parish register, Emma leaned over and whispered in his ear, "Does your grandmother know her solicitor is sweet on her?"

"What?" Henry stared at Emma, his eyes wide. "But he must be at least sixty!"

She nodded and smirked. "Age does not stop people from falling in love, you know."

Henry shook his head, not sure he felt capable of dealing with this revelation. He had just gotten married. He did not have the mental capacity to think about his grandmother's love life. What would happen to his mother if grandmother remarried? Would his grandmother move in with Mr. Beverly, or would Mr. Beverly move in with her? He rather suspected that Grandmother's house was the better one, but since he was not on visiting terms with Mr. Beverly, he could not be sure.

He kept shooting suspicious looks at Mr. Beverly while Emma took her turn to sign the registry, signing her maiden name for the last time.

"Henry," Emma whispered as she took his arm. "It is not your problem to solve."

"Oh." Henry stood stock still for a moment as he absorbed that idea. Emma had the right of it. Grandmother was an adult, after all. She had managed her own life quite well in the fifteen years since Grandfather Fletcher's death. She did not need Henry's supervision.

The newlyweds walked out of the church to the merry pealing of wedding bells. Henry wondered who had paid the bellringers to ring a peal for them. He thought it a needless extravagance, himself. It might have been his grandmother's doing. She had wanted the most lavish celebration possible under such short notice.

"But do you want me to tell your grandmother about his infatuation? She might not know." Emma spoke in a whisper.

Henry looked over at his grandmother. Mr. Beverly was thoughtfully helping her down the stairs. His grandmother smiled at the solicitor.

"No, don't tell her. If he wants her to know his feelings, he can tell her himself." Perhaps Mr. Beverly had no intention of acting on his infatuation. He might prefer to love from afar.

And anyway, Henry had other things to think about just now. Such as his bride. Most likely, Henry and Emma would have only a little time to themselves in which to decide how best to make a reconciliation with

Emma's family, assuming that such a thing was even possible. Much as Henry had enjoyed his fantasy of living with Emma in poverty and supporting her with his own labor, he knew they would have to return to Westwinds. Emma had responsibilities there, especially now that her uncle no longer had any control over the estate.

Henry would not mind living there. It was a pleasant house, and he could go back to translating that Ayles family spellbook. He would be doing a good deal of translating in the coming months, as it happened. Mr. Beverly had put him in touch with the magic mistress of a girl's school located just outside Scarborough. The magic mistress knew Latin, but most of her pupils did not, and thus they did not have access to many of the advanced spellbooks, which were commonly written in Latin. Vernacular spellbooks generally covered only elementary magic.

Miss Gardiner wanted Henry to translate intermediate manuals on sorcery and witchcraft for the use of her pupils. His own magical training made him ideal for such a task, since he understood the importance of properly translating magical terminology. A mundane Latin instructor, though better at the language, would not understand the spells as well as Henry did. This task would likely occupy Henry for months, if not longer. He would have paying work that could be done from Westwinds. Really, it seemed quite ideal.

In any case, it was not the return to Westwinds that made him anxious. Rather, he dreaded the confrontation with Emma's family. He did not believe he had done any wrong in marrying Emma. Being of age, Emma could marry when and where she wanted, without needing anyone's permission. Not only had Henry been handpicked as a suitor by her guardian, but the marriage itself had been perfectly above board.

The only irregularity in the matter was the way Emma had slunk out in the middle of the night. But a grown woman was entitled to leave her own home when she wanted to, wasn't she? So Henry told himself. But he suspected that Emma's aunt and uncle saw the matter differently, and he preferred to defer meeting them as long as he could.

His mother and grandmother, though they often quarreled, were both in agreement that Henry and Emma ought not spend their honeymoon in a crowded townhouse. Whether they were worried about the sensibilities of the newlyweds or about what his innocent younger siblings might overhear, Henry did not know, but either way, the result was that Grandmother paid for him and Emma to spend a week in lodgings overlooking the sea. Henry hoped that getting away from Princess Street might make it harder for Uncle Elwood to track them down.

The lodging house proved to be a quiet building at the edge of town, a little removed from the more fashionable streets. That made it ideal for Emma, who would not have liked a busy, crowded inn. When they arrived in their room after a laid-back wedding breakfast—thrown together at the last minute, because Grandmother insisted they must have one—the other guests were all out and about or quietly napping.

As Henry took his boots off, he stared at the large bed in the center of the room. The blue-white-and-green quilt pattern seemed familiar, though he had no idea what it was called. He swallowed nervously. They had had very little time together in the last thirty-six hours. He had meant to have a serious discussion about how their marriage would work while they were on the road from Westwinds to Scarborough, but somehow they had spent most of that time kissing. And groping. And...well, they had been somewhat preoccupied.

"Do you need to rest?" Henry tore his eyes away from the bed so he could look at Emma. "You were up early this morning."

Emma stared fixedly at the bed, too. Was she thinking the same thing he was? Rather than blushing or demurring, she looked up at him and smiled so bewitchingly that he bent his head down to kiss her lightly. She turned to face him, pressing her body against his, and opened her mouth to invite him to kiss her further. They had already stumbled to the bed before he realized she had never answered his question.

Henry had been kissing her at the place where her neck met her shoulder, but he paused now so he could talk. "Do you want to do this now? Or had you rather rest?" He desired her ravenously, but he could wait if she needed rest. He knew she had found her short stay with his family exhausting, though she had never complained.

"I do not need to rest," Emma gasped. "I need you." She reached up to place her hands on either side of Henry's face. "I missed you so very much, you know."

"I hope you are not going to make me grovel more," Henry grumbled.

During the brief periods of time in their carriage ride when they had not been kissing, he had employed his mouth in apologies and explanations. Emma had informed him, in colorful language, that he must have been lacking in both common sense and human sensibility to have run away despite being in love with her. She had also explained that he had been wrong to think his inability to keep his shields up meant they could not marry. This left Henry feeling more like a fool than ever, but at least she had accepted his apologies.

Emma smiled at him naughtily. "There might be other reasons for you to be on your knees."

Henry's eyes widened in shock at this suggestion. "What have you been reading?" Did her grandfather's library contain an unexpected trove of pornography?

"I have been doing some research." Emma's eyes danced with mischief as she unbuttoned Henry's navy-blue topcoat.

He shrugged the coat off and tossed it onto the floor. A tiny part of his mind worried the coat would get dirty. But most of his mind was focused on the way Emma's fingers undid the buttons on his white waistcoat. He removed his cravat himself, guessing it might be difficult for her to untie the knot. Then he was left in nothing but his breeches, his stockings, and his linen shirt. Emma reached up to pull his shirt off, but he stopped her.

"Don't I get to undress you?"

"If you can," she said doubtfully. "Do you even know how to unfasten a woman's dress?"

"How hard can it be?" Even the silliest of young women seemed capable of dressing themselves; surely, he could do it.

He felt triumphant when he undid the fastening on the dress. But then, after he had pulled the dress off, he was faced with her short stays. Emma laughed at his puzzled expression.

"How do these work?" he had to ask.

She took pity on him and unlaced her stays herself,

so all that was left was the white shift underneath. Henry reached for the hem, to pull that off, too, then paused. "Will you let me see you now?" Before, she had not wanted him to see her naked. But this was no longer a one-time *affaire* or summer fling. She was his wife now.

Emma chewed her thumbnail as she thought. He gave her space to think, instead occupying himself with pulling out all her hairpins. He was rather surprised by how many there were. Her hair tumbled down in long brown waves, and he watched, fascinated, as it framed her face. Somehow, she looked more bewitching than ever with her hair down.

"You really want to see my body?" Emma's voice sounded uncharacteristically small. Henry looked her in the eyes, seeing tension written in the lines of her face.

"Only if you don't mind. You can keep your shift on, if you prefer." She nodded, looking relieved. But something compelled him to whisper, "But I do *want* to see you, very much." He was so close he could hear her gulp.

"Very well," she whispered, and she herself lifted the shift off.

She did have a few pockmarks on her trunk and limbs, though they were neither as close together or as deep as the ones on her face. But the scars could not conceal the beauty of her body.

Emma wore one thing still, a wooden heart, hanging on a frail silver chain. "What's this?" Henry asked. The moment he touched it, his eyes widened as something tingled against the tips of his fingers. "A charm?" He did not recognize the spell.

Emma nodded. "That is the contraceptive charm I bought from the midwife," she said matter-of-factly. "Do you want me to take it off now that we are married?"

Henry's heart lurched in his chest, and his mouth went dry. She was asking him if he wanted to be a father. That would be even more responsibility than being a son, a brother, or a husband. A throng of uneasy thoughts and fears rioted together in his mind. His desire dwindled in the face of that anxiety.

"Keep it on for now, please. We can talk about it later." There was no reason why they could not have a child, but he had rather not worry about that just yet.

Emma nodded, and if she felt at all disappointed, she hid her disappointment well. Setting that question aside as best he could, Henry went back to studying his bride's body. He cupped her breasts reverently with his hands, exploring their shape. He was equally fascinated by the softness of the breasts and the firmness of her nipples. Emma caught her breath when he ran a thumb across her nipple.

"Does that hurt?" Henry had no idea how women's breasts felt to them, though he certainly liked the way they felt in his hands.

Emma shook her head. "It feels good."

He kept exploring her body until she became impatient and insisted that he remove the rest of his clothing too. At the back of his mind, it occurred to him that they were lucky this was a temperate day. How did people get naked in winter and still keep warm? Did they have to stay tucked beneath the covers? And if so, didn't that make it difficult to find things? Then Emma reached down to stroke his erection, and he ceased such pointless speculations. All that mattered was this moment when Emma was his to worship.

Loving Emma was certainly easier now that he was

no longer confined to one position, with his leg in an immovable cast. As she lay on the bed, he explored every supple curve and angle of her body. Mindful of her provocative suggestion, when he came to the cleft between her legs, he teased her with his lips and tongue as well as his hands.

"That feels good," Emma told him, "but do what you did with your thumb last time. That was better."

Henry found a pleasure of his own in watching her changing expression as she drew closer and closer to spending herself. She came with a gasp and a moan, grabbing his free hand and clutching it tightly. When she finished, Henry pulled her hand to his mouth so he could kiss the back of it.

"That was very good," she said.

He did not need mind magic to read the satisfaction in her face and voice. He felt a warm glow of pride at the thought that *he* had put that expression on her face. To make a wildcat purr like a kitten was surely a significant accomplishment.

Then Emma looked at him. "How do you want to do this? The same way we did last time, or—"

"No!" That came out more strongly than he intended, and Emma's eyes flew open wide. "If I never have to lie on my back in bed again, it will be too soon," he explained. He still had not gotten over the awful tedium of being trapped in bed for over a month. "Can I be on top this time?"

That might not be very creative, but it *was* traditional. Emma nodded and opened her legs wider for him. He still needed her help guiding himself inside her. He hoped that would grow easier in time. But then they were joined, and he let himself once again stop thinking of everything but the sensation—and Emma herself.

Henry propped himself up on his elbows, not wanting Emma to have to bear his full weight. In this position, he felt very aware of how much smaller she was, compared to him. The top of her head did not even reach his chin, and his broadly built frame dwarfed hers.

"How does this feel? I'm not hurting you, am I?" He vaguely felt his heaviness might make things painful.

But Emma shook her head. "Of course not, silly. It didn't hurt the first time. Why would it hurt now?"

She lifted her upper body so she could kiss him, though he had to bend his head down to reach her. Then she rocked her hips, and he happily put aside his anxieties to focus on the delightful way their bodies joined together. He had optimistically hoped that perhaps this time he would last longer, but once again things ended rather sooner than he liked. He hardly felt like complaining, though, as he gave himself up to the too-brief sensation of pulsating release.

This time, he forgot to even *try* to keep his mental shields up, and he could hear Emma echoing his pleasure as her body responded to the sensations her mind picked up. Evidently, it would take more practice if he wanted to keep his mind closed off during such moments. But he was not entirely sure he did want that. He rather liked the idea that they were psychically joined at the same time as they were physically joined. It would, he supposed, be up to Emma to decide. The smile on her face suggested she had no complaints.

Henry let himself rest in her arms for a while before moving to lie next to her. "I might take that nap now," she said with a yawn.

"Me too," he murmured, and he fell asleep, still

holding his bride.

Chapter Twenty-Two

Henry must have woken from his nap first, because when Emma opened her eyes, she lay in bed alone. She sat up and looked about, puzzled. His clothes, which had lain scattered all over the floor, were gone, so she assumed he must have gotten dressed and left. Perhaps he had gone for a walk? That did not seem like him, though. A chill of foreboding traveled down her spine. She told herself not to be superstitious. She did not have the ability to predict the future.

Still, she got up and dressed in a hurry. She put on her walking dress, rather than that ridiculously ornate wedding gown, and she wrapped her hair up in a hasty bun. She was in such a hurry to find Henry that she did not realize she had left her hat and veil behind until she was already halfway down the stairs from their suite to the ground floor. Well, it was too late to get it now.

She heard Henry's voice, surprisingly loud, coming from the central hall. Yes, she saw him as she rounded the curve of the stairs. He was arguing with a man just a little shorter than he was. In a fraction of a second, Emma recognized the man's voice, and her heart sank.

"I hope you do not think you can get away with this," Uncle Elwood spat at Henry. "I cannot believe I was so wrong about you, Mr. Dawson. I will see you in court, and I will see this fraudulent marriage dissolved, if it is the last thing I do!"

"On what grounds?" Henry snapped back. "Your niece is of age. The marriage was perfectly legal and has already been consummated, so—" What Henry meant to say next would never be known, because Uncle Elwood struck him in the face.

"Uncle Elwood!" Emma galloped down the last step and raced to interpose herself between her husband and her former guardian. "How dare you hit my husband!"

"Emma!" Uncle Elwood shook out his hand, as if it had gone numb. "I will speak to you later, young lady. First, I need to deal with this cad—"

"No." Emma crossed her arms in front of her chest and stood up to her full height. She was a little above average height for a woman, and usually she was quite content with that, but just now she wished she were tall enough to stand eye to eye with her uncle. "There is nothing you need to deal with here, Uncle. I am very sorry, but we are on our honeymoon. When the week is up, we will come back to Westwinds, and you can speak to us at your leisure. But my husband and I are not receiving visitors now, so you will have to leave."

Her uncle stared at her. Then he looked at Henry, whose usually friendly face had gone hard as marble. Perhaps a punch to the cheekbone had that effect on him. Uncle Elwood's eyes flicked back to Emma, and now he looked puzzled.

"Emma, you may think you are legally married, but are you sure that everything is in order?" Uncle Elwood shook his head anxiously. "I cannot help but feel there must be some trick here, and—"

"*Uncle*," Emma said, speaking as firmly as she could. "I saw the license myself. It had the bishop's signature. We were married in Henry's parish church this morning by a clergyman of the Church of England. Everything was in proper order."

"But if everything was in order, why on earth did you elope this way? Emma, you ran off in the middle of the night! Your aunt was terrified that you had been kidnapped!" Uncle Elwood's voice sounded plaintive rather than angry now. He must have been very scared.

"I left a note." Emma wished she could have kept that rock-hard tone of certainty, but her voice wavered now, too. "I explained that I was running off to get married."

She sighed. Had it been wrong of her to run off like that? She was an adult now, true, but that did not mean she needed to frighten her family. She opened her mouth to apologize to her uncle, but Henry reached out and wrapped his arm about her waist, pulling her closer to him.

"Sir, you have heard your niece." He spoke calmly and politely now. "This is our honeymoon. We do not choose to be disturbed just now. We can make our explanations at Westwinds this day week. I look forward to seeing you then, Uncle Elwood."

He nodded his head. Then he turned and led her away. Emma glanced back over her shoulder to see her uncle standing still, looking confused and crestfallen. Her heart ached at his expression. Part of her wanted to run back and smooth things over, but she thought a little time apart might make reconciliation easier. Instead of turning back to her childhood guardian, she looked ahead as she walked away with Henry.

The rest of the week passed much less eventfully. Emma and Henry went for walks every day. Twice, they hired a fisherman to take them out on the water in a skiff so they could enjoy the view of the land from the sea. Emma made Henry shop for new clothing, since he admitted he had not had so much as a new waistcoat or nightshirt in two years. She had brought enough money with her from Westwinds to at least buy a few new shirts, cravats, and nightshirts. They could get him more clothes in Whitby, later.

And they spent a considerable amount of time in bed. Henry desired her just as fiercely as ever, and perhaps some of his ardor rubbed off on Emma, because she found she had just as strong an appetite for carnal delights. She had enjoyed going to bed with Henry from the start, but it seemed to get better and better as they gradually acquired more experience. She kept her contraceptive charm on, though, because she could see that something about the prospect of having children troubled him.

It was not until their weeklong holiday was nearly over that he opened up about that. They had taken a picnic luncheon out to the beach. At first the beach was full of children playing, but soon clouds blocked the sun, and many of the holiday trippers left, giving Henry and Emma some privacy. Emma knew that soon enough they would have to walk back to their lodgings, if for no other reason than that she needed to use the water closet, but for now it was pleasant to sit next to her husband and listen to the roar of the waves as the tide retreated.

They had been sitting in silence, watching seagulls circling overhead, when Henry spoke. "We should come here with our children someday."

"I would like that." Emma looked up at him uncertainly. "I thought perhaps you did not want children." It was one of the many things they had never

233

had time to properly discuss, given their elopement.

He looked down at her and smiled briefly, then reached out to take her hand. "I like children well enough. But it is a frightening thing to be responsible for such tender lives. I suppose I must be a coward after all."

"Frightening?" Emma wrinkled her brow as she tried to puzzle that out.

"So many things can go wrong. And children demand so much of one." Henry looked away from her, out over the ocean. "I used to be angry at my father for dying," he said, apropos of nothing. "It was a heart attack, yes, so I know he could not help it, but I hated that he escaped his responsibilities and left me to bear them. I had only just turned two-and-twenty, and I expected my life to be very different."

Emma squeezed his hand tightly. He had his mental shields up, so she could not sense his emotions, but she could hear a great deal of pain in his voice.

He shrugged his shoulders, looked down at her, and smiled ruefully. "You have met my mother. Your uncle would say that she has no *rumgumption*. When Father died, she fell apart. From grief, yes, but also from shock when she learned how much debt he had accumulated."

"Anyone would fall apart from that," Emma said. "Two great shocks at once."

She did not want to say much more, not having had the chance to do more than make the acquaintance of Mrs. Dawson. She *had* carried away the distinct impression that it was Henry's grandmother who provided the backbone and the brains of the household. Perhaps "rumgumption," like magic, sometimes skipped a generation.

"Yes, but you see, I was not allowed to fall apart."

Henry sat with his knees propped up, and now he took his hand away from Emma's so he could wrap both arms around his legs, hugging himself tightly. "I inherited the estate after Father's death, so I was the one responsible for most of the financial decisions. When we decided to sell Switherton to pay off the debt, I was the one who had to sign it over. The creditors all wanted to talk to me, not my mother. Even though I was hardly more than a boy."

Emma nodded. She had experienced that, too, but in reverse. Men of business did not want to correspond with her, because she was a girl. They assumed that business decisions must be handled by the man in her life, whoever that might be.

"I had to find new schools for Eliza and Jasper—schools good enough for the children of a gentleman but cheap enough for a family in reduced circumstances. Do you know how hard that was to do?" He sighed. "I don't know where we would be if Grandmother had not been able to take Mother in. Or rather, I do know. We'd be living in some little cottage or cheap flat, and Mother would do an even worse job of making ends meet. There would be no way to send the children to school."

Emma reached out to put her hand on his shoulder. Her husband looked so strong, but just now he sounded vulnerable. "Henry, you did your best, I know. And you need not worry about Jasper and Eliza now. We can afford—"

To her surprise, he shook his head. "No. I will earn the money to send Jasper and Eliza to school. You should not have to pay for that. That is my responsibility, not yours."

Emma swallowed, feeling a lump form in her throat. "But your family is mine now," she protested. "We are married."

Henry turned to her and took her face in his hands. "Yes, we are married," he agreed, his deep blue eyes looking soft and tender. "But I want no one to think I married you for your fortune. I married you because I love you, Emma."

Emma closed her eyes at those words, thinking of all the many times she had grieved because she thought she would only be loved for her inheritance. The tears burning behind her eyelids now were not tears of sorrow, but a response to a pang so sweet that it hurt.

"I will do my best to support my family. Save your money for *our* children." He kissed her tenderly on the mouth, just brushing his lips lightly against hers. Emma leaned forward to kiss him back.

Then someone whistled, and Emma's eyes flew open. She had entirely forgotten they still sat on a public beach. Though many of the families had gone home, a few people remained. A group of half-grown boys stood some yards away, giggling at the sight of two grownups kissing on the beach.

"Get out of here!" Henry called at the children, but then he started laughing, and the boys laughed even harder in response. Emma pulled her veil over her face to hide the blush that burned her cheeks. She hoped the veil granted her some dignity.

"Perhaps," she suggested, "we ought to go back to our rooms."

"Yes," Henry agreed, still chuckling. "I think our picnic is over." He gave her a hand up, and they headed back.

Henry limped just a little on the way home, suggesting that he felt tired. He had been doing well without crutches or cane, and she had some hope that he would make a full recovery. Bastian had already healed, so perhaps soon enough that dreadful accident would be only a memory. Which reminded Emma that when they got back to Westwinds they would have to look for a hack sturdy enough for Henry, one that did not shy at the sound of thunder.

They rolled up to Westwinds in a hired chaise on a sunny afternoon in August. Henry helped Emma out of the chaise, took their luggage out, and sent the postilions on their way. Emma stood staring at her home, with its handsome battlements and narrow, old-fashioned windows. It looked exactly the same as it always had. She was the one who had changed.

"We had better go face the music," Henry said grimly.

Before they even reached the entrance, Aunt Mary flung the door open and ran out to greet them, as if the prodigal had returned. "Oh, my dear!" she called.

As usual, Aunt Mary did not properly shield her mind, so Emma felt the full brunt of her aunt's happiness, relief, and just a touch of sadness. She wondered what Aunt Mary had to be sad about. Then her aunt's arms were around her. To Emma's dismay, she found her aunt weeping on her shoulder.

"Oh, Emma, you gave me such a turn! I thought my heart would break when I woke up and found you gone. To think of you running off to get married on your own, and never telling me a peep about it!"

Oh, so that was it—Aunt Mary felt hurt because Emma had gotten married without her. Somehow, this was a reaction Emma had not anticipated. She had expected her family to be angry. She had not realized they would be hurt at being left out. Was that how Uncle Elwood felt, too? She embraced her aunt tightly, feeling the full weight of her emotional pain for a moment. Then she stepped back.

"Shields, Aunt Mary, please," she begged, her voice wavering a little.

"Oh, yes, I am so sorry." Aunt Mary stepped back, too, and tried her best to keep her emotions to herself. She was no more successful than usual, but her unhappiness felt more tolerable now that Emma was no longer touching her.

"Aunt Mary," Emma said formally. "I am very sorry. I ought not to have run away. I—" Her voice broke. "I don't know what I was thinking."

"Miss Barker," Henry said, bowing over Aunt Mary's hand with the grace of a courtier, "it was my fault entirely. I led Emma astray, simply because I was too impatient to have her as my bride. I can only plead a lovestruck heart in my defense. Can you forgive me?" He smiled charmingly, and then, to Emma's vast amusement, kissed her aunt's hand.

"Oh!" Aunt Mary blushed and stepped back, overcome by this sudden display of gallantry. "Well! Young love will always be unpredictable."

Through her empathy, Emma picked up the sense that her aunt had been both charmed and flustered by Henry's explanation of the elopement. Aunt Mary was momentarily at a loss for words, and Henry used this as a chance to continue making peace.

"Let us let bygones be bygones," he said, cheerfully ignoring the fact that all the faults were on his and Emma's side. "And start fresh. May I call you 'Aunt'?" It sounded as if calling her "Aunt" had long been the deepest desire of his heart.

"Of course." Aunt Mary smiled. "Now come inside and get tidied up. I will get you some refreshments."

And that, to Emma's surprise, was the last Aunt Mary said about Emma's scandalous elopement. From thereon after, she treated Emma and Henry's marriage as a settled fact, and even happily chatted to Henry about the woodland motif they had chosen for the border in his bedroom.

Emma had only been away from home for a little over a week, but coming home to Westwinds still felt strange. Some of it was the fact that she now occupied the bedroom that had once been her mother's. She peered into her old room, just out of curiosity, and saw that all her possessions had been moved out. The bed had been stripped, the curtains taken down. The room stood empty of personality, ready to be filled by a houseguest…or, perhaps, a daughter of her own someday. When Henry was ready.

She found Henry hanging up some of his clothes in the wardrobe in the newly dubbed Ivy Room. "We should get you some new evening clothes," she suggested cheerfully. He looked good in almost any shade of blue, but she liked him in black and white, too.

"Not until I get paid for my first translation job," he replied. "It was kind of you to buy me some new things as a wedding gift, but from now on, I will pay for my own clothes."

Emma stared at him. For a moment, she could not identify the emotion that swirled inside her. She had been so full of strong emotions today, from anxiety to regret to that curiously bittersweet feeling of looking at her home and finding that she had in some ways outgrown it. This emotion was one she had not felt in days. It made her clench her fists, tighten her jaw, and tip up her chin.

Oh, but she was *angry*. "Henry Dawson, you are a stubborn fool!"

Chapter Twenty-Three

Henry felt his jaw drop from shock. His wife had just insulted him. To his face. While he stood in his own bedroom, in the house they now shared. Was the honeymoon over? They would fight like cats and dogs, he had predicted. Looks like he had been right. He should have known.

He glanced away, angrily working his jaw as he tried to think how to respond. From her perspective, what he had just said probably seemed inexplicable. "Emma, I love you," he began. "But I will not be your kept man. I do not want to be dependent on you. I thought you knew that."

Emma crossed her arms in front of her chest and looked up at him, her chin tilted at a defiant angle. "Henry," she said, in the voice parents use when their patience begins to wear thin, "you are not a kept man. You are my husband. In the eyes of the law, we are one. And in the marriage ceremony, you promised to endow me with all your worldly goods, so it is only fair if I do the same."

"But *you* didn't vow to endow *me* with your worldly goods," Henry retorted. "Only the husband makes that promise. Because it is a husband's job to provide for his family."

"Oh, Henry." Emma's voice sounded soft and tender now, and it pierced Henry to the heart. So did the appealing look she gave him—was that what people meant when they talked about the pleading eyes of a puppy dog? Her brown eyes were certainly as soft and beseeching as those of a spaniel begging for table scraps. "You worked so hard to support your family when your father died. You should be proud of that. But you don't have to do that anymore. We can support them together."

Emma stepped closer to him and reached out to touch his face. Her fingers brushed against his cheek, feeling both warm and soft, and he almost reached up to take her hand and kiss it. Almost.

Henry stared down at her, wavering. Then he shook his head. "I understand that we will live off your inheritance. I know that Westwinds is what will feed us, and Westwinds is yours. It always will be, whatever the law might say. But Emma, you must allow me some pride. I must be allowed to do my part." She furrowed her brow and gnawed on her thumbnail. He recognized that gesture. She was weakening. "I will purchase my own clothes," he told her, "from what I can earn myself."

Emma lifted her chin again, signaling an attack. "And how do you think I will feel, seeing you go about in shabby clothes from two seasons ago? People will say I am a skinflint."

"How do you think I feel when people say that I am a fortune hunter? That I married you only to get Westwinds?"

Emma scowled. "How do you know people say that? Have you heard them?"

Henry ran a hand through his hair, half-wishing he could yank it out in frustration. "I don't need to hear them to know what they're saying." Everyone would assume that about him, once they knew Henry's story.

And they probably already knew his story, given how fast gossip traveled in small towns.

"So what if they say it?" Emma continued. "If I were a man, and you a woman, no one would think anything of me marrying you, even if you were poor. They would say it was a love match, and that it was just like a fairy tale. If there is nothing wrong with a rich man marrying a poor girl out of love, what could be wrong with me marrying you? Because our marriage is a love match...isn't it?"

The tiny hint of doubt in her voice went straight to his heart. Henry put his arms around her and leaned forward to kiss her on the forehead. "Of course it is a love match. I married you because I couldn't be happy without you." Emma stepped closer and rested her head on his chest, willing to be consoled.

If Henry had stopped talking then, all would have been well. But some evil genius compelled him to add, "It is just a little different when the impoverished partner is a man, love. Women are expected to be dependent, but men—"

"Are pigheaded fools?" Emma stepped out of his embrace and stomped her foot. "What's sauce for the goose is sauce for the gander. There is nothing wrong with you being dependent on me. You are just too proud to accept my gift."

Before he could answer her, she turned on her heel and stormed out of the room. At least she shut the door gently. He had to give her that. He had been half afraid she would slam it behind her.

Henry sighed and buried his face in his hands for a moment. He understood why Emma might want to shower him with gifts now they were married. If the shoe had been on the other foot, he would have delighted in clothing her with diamonds and silk. Any man would want to see his bride look her best. No doubt Emma merely wanted the same for him.

But he meant what he said. He wanted to do his best to pay his own way, even if his best was the merest mite. He would not be able to earn much from translating spellbooks into English, but it would be honest work. He could not be content living the life of a lapdog. He was leaving the management of Westwinds to Emma—and who better could there be to manage it?—and therefore he must have his own employment.

It was only as he paced back and forth in his room, going over all the arguments he wanted to make, that it occurred to him that he could, after all, work on his translations and still accept Emma's charity. Though "charity" might be the wrong word to use, given that she was his wife. Their lives, their home, and their future were one. Why not their finances, as well?

If Henry and Emma had been a poor couple living in a tiny flat in town, as he had once fantasized they might be, they would both have labored to support themselves, together, as a unit. In such a case, he would not have been ashamed to touch the money Emma earned. Was it so very different now? If he could have accepted her help in the one scenario, why not in the other?

He experienced a shiver of foreboding that he recognized from the past. He felt suddenly certain that Emma was going to win this argument in the end. She usually did win, because she was more persistent than he was. She would wear him down with her logic, then destroy him with her emotion.

It would all end with her buying new evening clothes for him. She would probably even get the final say about the pattern of his waistcoats and the color of his breeches. At least, he thought ruefully, she had good taste. He did not have to worry about her picking out things that did not suit him.

Yes, Emma would probably have her way in the end. But by God, he thought with a grin, he was going to go down fighting! He whistled as he went to look for his wife, to tell her how wrong she was.

A word about the author...

Anne Rollins is the pen name of an English professor who lives in Northern California with her family, her pets, and an enormous collection of books. She is equally a fan of Diana Wynne Jones and Georgette Heyer, two authors whose writing influenced this novel. She also writes children's books under the name Teresa Traver. This is her first novel.

Visit her at:

annerollins.com